"Drawn to intrigue, once again, I quickly became caught up in a Patty Wiseman novel! I dove into the sequel, An Unlikely Beginning, and couldn't lay the book down! Patty delivered unexpected twists and turns, totally surpassing what I'd hoped for! Great work and well written! Can't wait for the third book in the series!"
Lynn Hobbs
Award Winning Author, *Sin, Secrets, and Salvation*

"Picking up with the mystery of shootings and murder, the continuing story of An Unlikely Arrangement couldn't have come out fast enough! Written with such drama and emotion, I felt as if I was struggling with the life changing decisions along with Ruth. There are so many twists and turns that you never want to stop reading. Such a great story! I would recommend it to all. There is love, history, tragedy, mystery, and hope, all tangled together in this intriguing drama. I laughed, cried, cheered, and gasped throughout the entire book!"
Kimberly Farmer
Panola College instructor

"Once again, Patty Wiseman delivers vivid imagery and heart-searing emotion...This sequel's tantalizing suspense will pull you deeper into the story until each answer is unveiled, a nugget at a time, in a way that never fails to surprise. Patty's knowledge of people's characters and reactions to life's traumas give the books a deep and believable appeal. An Unlikely Arrangement and An Unlikely Beginning, once started, are hard to put down."
Eva Blaskovic
Author, Beyond the Precipice and The Waiting Room,

"What do you do with a series of good books? Like a Klondike Bar, you gobble them up. And that's exactly what I plan to do. Will you do the same?"
Kevin Gray
Marshall High School teacher

For Dyani,
Best wishes!..
Patty Wiseman

An Unlikely Beginning

About the Author:

The daughter of a WWII Navy vet who survived Pearl Harbor, Patty Wiseman was raised in Washington State, attended The Wesleyan College in Bartlesville, Oklahoma, and eventually moved to Northeast Texas where she has resided for over 30 years.

Writing has been a life-long passion and in 2007, she entered the NaNoWriMo competition to write a novel in 30 days and won, attempted it again in 2011 and completed it again. Several of her short stories are published and two more novels are in the works. She is the creator of the Velvet Shoe Collection of Romantic Mysteries.

She has two grown sons, eleven grandchildren and a beautiful step-daughter.

Patty currently lives in Texas with her wonderful husband Ron and their crème lab Cutter.

Also by Patty Wiseman:
The Velvet Shoe Collection
    An Unlikely Arrangement

An Unlikely Beginning

Patty Wiseman

Desert Coyote Productions
Scotts Valley, California

Library of Congress Control Number 2012939954.
EAN-13: 978-1-477-40890-2
ISBN-10: 1-477-40890-8

Typeset in 11pt Book Antiqua
Printed in the U.S.A.

To my father, Calvin Clifford Dawes, who never knew his father, a truly remarkable man; because of modern technology I have the privilege of bringing him to life.

Acknowledgments

First and foremost thanks go to my husband of 20 years, Ron Wiseman, a man who never wavers in his devotion and support.

In this world, we are blessed with those we love and who love us. Two people I have cherished since the day they were born are my two sons, Lance Cameron and Scott Cameron. No matter the trial, no matter the heartache, a mother's love is unconditional.

To Lance, a journey, untold revelations, and despite life's hardships, remembers…

To Scott, my rock, my advice giver, a huge support, and a shoulder when I need it.

To my mother, Lola Dawes, who at 87, cannot read anymore, but who has her friends read my books to her. Yes, Mom, I'm working on the audio book.

To Lynn Hobbs, a friend and critique partner, a good listener, an upbeat person who never wavers in her support.

To all the friends who read the first book and encouraged me to write the series. You are too numerous to list, but you know who you are.

Contents

An Unlikely Beginning

Chapter One

In the far corner of a seedy speakeasy known as the Blue Feather, seventeen year old Ruth Squire tried to avoid the interested eye of a repugnant patron. The impatient bartender waved his hand toward the stage—it was her turn to sing, but the metallic taste of fear drenched her tongue and slithered downward until her stomach burned. She took a step back.

A female voice whispered from behind, "Remember why we are doing this Ruthie. You can't abandon him now."

Slowly, courage overtook the fear. One step—another, until she stood center stage. The piano began the prelude, and she closed her eyes. A few tremulous notes exhaled through ruby lips, but strengthened as memories of the murderous carnage at home unfolded and steeled her will. The choice to save him was hers. Instead of a pack of crude, bawdy men in a smoke filled room, she envisioned Peter, the man she came to rescue. Her eyes opened, and she remembered…

Late Friday afternoon, February 1929

A shard of light punctured the somber, country scene, a flash that vanished so quickly, Ruth Squire wondered if it was imagination or reality. The next instant, a well-dressed man emerged from behind a far off willow tree and disappeared down the dirt road, alone. From that distance, she couldn't tell his age, but noticed the black fedora hat, the dark suit, and shiny black shoes. In light of the recent murders, not only in Detroit proper, but even in her own house, fear reminded her it wasn't over.

The snow fell silently, covering the dead grass, and dusting the grave stones in the antiquated cemetery on the edge of town. Winter decided to creep into the quiet necropolis as if to remind its temporary occupants who remained in charge. There was no rhyme or reason to this murder, no logical explanation, yet here they stood in front of a casket about to be lowered into the ground. Ruth's heels sank into the lifeless sod, but at her side, Peter Kirby gripped her elbow a bit tighter. She wanted to cry, tried to force it…almost willed the tears to spring forth, but when she blinked, the rough sandpaper she called eyelids dissolved any thread of emotion. So far, the year 1929 was a complete disaster.

The air was silent except for the forlorn cry of a faraway mourning dove. Ruth looked to the sky and felt tiny snowflakes kiss her numb cheeks. *We shouldn't be here, this shouldn't be happening. Whose bizarre idea was this, anyway?* She looked up into Peter's solemn face. A shiver ran through her and it was an automatic response to lean into him for warmth. The last thing she wanted to do was attend this funeral. Her heart was too raw, the pain too fresh. Surprised at the paltry attendance, she looked from one stone face to the next. *Why did they bother to come? Why did I?*

2

Finally, the last scripture was read, the last hymn was sung, and the ritual handfuls of dirt thumped against the wooden box deep in the hole. It's over.

Peter deftly steered her toward the automobile, settled her into the front seat, and wrapped a plaid, flannel blanket around both legs. She smiled at him for his thoughtfulness. Mother was right about him, at least. Maybe her motive to marry me off was skewed, but at least, it turned out to be the right choice…maybe. "Let's go straight home, Peter, I'm sure Father is feeling our absence. He was more than a little upset when I insisted he stay home. The guilt grows each day for my part in his pneumonia. Has it only been a few weeks since I tried to sneak out my bedroom window? Look at the havoc I've wreaked and the lives I've destroyed in such a short time."

"Ruth, I will not hear anymore talk of your blame. You were acting no different than any other young woman in your position. Do you think you were the first girl to sneak out of a window?" Peter squeezed her hand. "Think of it this way…we would never have met if you had let that window stifle your adventurous spirit." He smiled. "Your mother wouldn't have arranged the marriage between us. It could have been so much worse. We could have hated each other, had no attraction whatsoever. Let's not let all this unpleasantness tear us apart. We were meant to be together."

The grim landscape passed by in a kaleidoscope of white snowflakes. Ruth tried to make sense of the conflict in her soul. How can Peter think that? Mother and Sarah, shot. A strange man gunned down in the hallway, and who was the man at the door who ran away? Guilt played a continuous scene-by-scene silent movie of the past events in her head, leaving her exhausted and depressed. It was my fault, she thought. All of it.

It all appeared so innocent at the time. She was young, impulsive…adventurous. Sneaking out of bedroom windows was almost a rite of passage at seventeen or eighteen years old. Everyone did it. This time, something snapped in Mother and decided the solution to this insubordinate behavior was to marry her off to Peter Kirby. Appalled at the time, Ruth fought against it—until she saw him. Sun kissed hair, piercing blue eyes, athletic build. She fell hard for him, much to her surprise. Unfortunately, Hattie Morgenstern came to claim a childhood betrothal to Peter from their homeland. Once more, Ruth acted impulsively and ran away, setting in motion a series of sinister events.

My fault, I admit. I acted impulsively, once again. But am I to blame for Mother's plight? I am certainly not responsible for the actions of the scoundrel Captain Alexander Adams. All this insanity began long before I was born.

Peter spoke gently in her ear. "Ruth, we're home. I must see to my horses and the milk route. I will be back after I take care of the obligations." He helped her out of the automobile, and they walked hand in hand to the front door. "I know this isn't the proper time to talk about this, but in light of what's happened, I think we need to marry right away."

"Peter," she paused, heart torn, but unable to shake the remorse. "Talk of marriage is out of the question, tonight. My mind cannot process more. I think I want to be alone tonight — with Father. He is so ill. There's no one to tend him. I'm sorry, but…"

"Ruth, please, you do not have to explain. We're all exhausted. I want nothing more than for your father to recover. Take all the time you need. My own mother has been devastated. I'll call on you in a few days. We'll talk then." He bent to kiss her cheek.

"Thank you, Peter. I am all he has now." One hand remained clasped in his as a silent moment passed between them. She looked up again. "It is going to be alright, isn't it Peter?"

"Time is a great healer, my love. Things will return to a normal pace, I promise." Peter opened the front door and ushered her inside.

Imaginary lead weights clung to her feet as she trudged up the stairs. She stood by the bedroom window; the same window used for the doomed escape, and watched Peter drive away. Even after the automobile disappeared into the distance, she stood with the curtain pushed aside, and stared at nothing, thoughts tumbling. "How can I fix this? More importantly, how can I marry Peter with Father's life in shambles? I can't leave him. This house is too big, too empty…" A shiver coursed down her spine. "Can't think about that now. Father needs his medicine."

The chill in the hallway was a reminder the big drafty house was now her responsibility. Father must stay warm. She stopped in front of Mother's bedroom door. It was closed. "I wonder if I will ever be able to enter that room—the closet, the letters." Her fingers rested on the doorknob, and she could almost smell the fragrance of violets. If she opened the door, the scent would be her undoing. She continued down the hall to Father's room.

His feeble voice answered her knock with an almost inaudible "Come in", and she entered slowly. "Papa? How are you feeling?"

A hacking cough greeted the question.

She ran to the overstuffed chair and readjusted the heavy wool blanket around his shoulders and the lap quilt around both knees. He was shivering. "Father you are so cold. I should never have left you. I'll turn up the heat."

The coughing subsided, and Ruth watched him shake his head.

"No, daughter, I am fine. We can't afford the extra fuel. Leave it be. Maybe a fire would help, but I haven't the strength to fetch the wood." He stared vacantly at the stone hearth.

Ruth stood abruptly. "I can get the wood, but first you need your medicine."

While she filled the spoon with the elixir, he continued to protest. "It's no job for a girl. These blankets are warm enough, no need to strain yourself. It's not ladylike. Just fix me some hot soup, and I'll be right as rain in a day or two."

She stopped at the door and looked back. "Father, I can manage a few sticks of wood. Sarah always built the fires when things got a little chilly in the rooms. If she could do it, I can too. I'll build the fire, and then get right on your soup."

6

"It's no work for a young girl." Robert Squire patted his knee. "Ruthie, please come here. Tell me about the funeral. Were there many people? What about the service? I should have been there with you. You should never go unescorted."

Ruth returned to him, sat on the floor, and laid her head on his lap. "Peter was there. It was much too cold for you. Not many people attended. I wasn't surprised by that. The air was bitter. It's over, Father. We need to get on with our lives, now."

The wind rattled the glass panes; a gust of air escaped through the flue and sent a shiver through her body. "This old house. I think we may have to sell it, Father. It costs too much to keep it in good repair."

"I'll not leave this house, Ruthie. Your mother and I spent our entire married lives here. You were born in this house. I can hire help. You need to start your life; marry Peter."

The clock chimed the hour, and the light from the window faded to almost black. Ruth was reminded dinner would not cook itself, and the night air would bring more cold. She pushed up from the wood floor, hugged Father, and tightened the blanket around his shoulders. "Dinner needs to be addressed. I cannot sit here and coddle you." She kissed his forehead. "I'll be back with your soup and wood for a fire. There is no time to think of Peter when you need me so much."

He tried to protest, but Ruth closed the door softly. She knew, in her heart, she was the cause of all this tragedy in their lives. The shooting would never have occurred if she hadn't tried to go dancing with friends. So much was lost. There would be no marriage to

Peter. In less than a month, she had changed from a girl to a woman, from a self-centered child to the lady of the house. Responsibility loomed like an anvil ready to drop and crush the life out of her.

The kitchen welcomed her, warm and cozy, but did little to assuage the tumult deep in her soul. The soup stock bubbled on the stove, the steam warmed her face, and the freshly cleaned vegetables disappeared, one by one, into the hearty broth as the large knife clicked against the wooden cutting board. Was it only a few days ago? How can life continue to march ahead?

The scene at the wharf blazed a knife track through her brain. It played a vivid tableau, over and over. She would never be free of it. They were all there. Cal Taylor, her friend from Barkley's Women's School, Hattie Morgenstern, fresh from Holland to honor a childhood betrothal to Peter, the man *Ruth* wanted to marry. The extortionist banker, Eric Horton—found dead in the river—his body dragged from its murky depths. Never in her life had she witnessed such a thing, and she remembered every detail. Cal's worried voice saying he saw a gunman in the window. Peter dragging her back to the car, the mad chase behind Cal and Hattie, Father's shaken voice, almost in tears, as he realized his wife was at home, alone; the set of Peter's jaw as he fought to keep up with the others.

The autos pulled in front of the house. At first, they all shouted at each other, trying frantically to open the doors, but Peter saw it first and hushed everyone.

In a flat tone, he announced, "The door is open. We're too late."

Ruth whispered beside him. "What does it mean?"

The air split with the sound of a gunshot, and then another. A man ran out and disappeared down the alleyway.

Peter and Cal jumped from the automobiles and bounded up the steps, Robert Squire close behind. Peter stopped at the top step, pointed at the women, and shouted. "Stay where you are."

Ruth watched Father brush past Peter and disappear inside. An ear-piercing scream sent a bone-shattering chill through her. Both Cal and Peter entered the house, and moments later, returned with Father grasped between them, his head hanging, sobbing uncontrollably.

Terrified, Ruth ran to the men, shouting, "What is it, what happened?"

Hattie caught up and wrapped her arms around Ruth. She tried to wrench away, but Hattie held firm.

Peter held on to Robert with both hands, and Cal did the same. Father was hysterical.

"You cannot go in there, Ruth. It's complete devastation. We must call the police," Peter shouted.

She struggled against Hattie's grasp, but the taller woman held her fast. "But what of Mother? Please, tell me what happened. Where is Sarah?"

Neither man answered. Peter gave Robert over to Cal who continued across the lawn to the house next to the Squires, the women close behind. Cal pounded on the door until the lady of the house answered, white faced.

She opened the door only slightly. "I heard gunfire. What has happened? Is it the gangs again? Mr. Squire what is going on over there?"

"We'll explain later. Do you have a telephone? We need to call the police…and the hospital," Cal said.

The woman allowed them in, and the authorities were alerted. While they waited, Cal explained the scene inside the house. Three people were sprawled on the floor, Sarah the maid, Ruth's mother, and another man—a stranger.

Robert sobbed in the corner as Cal continued. "Peter went back to see what he can do for the wounded. Let's not think the worst until he brings us a report."

"Mother," Ruth whispered. "And Sarah." She went to her father to comfort him. "It will be fine, Father. They can't be dead. It will be alright, you'll see."

"You didn't see it, daughter. Blood all over, Mother lying on the floor, Sarah behind her. They are dead, both of them. I just know it."

They heard the sirens as two police cars screamed to a stop in front of the Squire's house. A few minutes later, Peter's shadow filled the doorway.

Ruth ran to him and pleaded, "Peter, what is the news. Are they dead? Please I have to know."

Peter took her in his arms. "I have good news and bad news, Ruth. Come and sit down."

Chapter Two

Shadowy remnants of the vegetable garden, withered stalks black and ghostly, forced the horrific memory to the background, allowing more pressing matters to drift to the surface. Ruth tapped the countertop with the wooden soup ladle and stared out the window at the patch of land, bedraggled, broken…lifeless.

Suddenly, she knew. It is the right thing to do. How can I go willy nilly into this marriage? People have been killed, and I think only of myself? I must tell Peter I cannot go through with this wedding. She accepted it, but continued to agonize over the thought of never seeing him again or experience the thrill of his touch. Father needs me more than ever. He has to be the focus now. There is nothing I can do for the others. The doctors made it clear no one was allowed at the hospital. The bullet lodged in Mother's chest, close to the heart. Any disturbance could cause the slug to move, possibly cause death, and poor Sarah was in a coma.

An acrid smell of scorched soup spun life back into the kitchen, and she rushed to stifle the overflow of hot liquid.

"Peter will have to understand. These things happened because I wanted to have fun, I was so selfish. Now, the people I love, and who love me, are suffering." Her jaw ached from tension, but now the decision was made. She clanged the tray against the counter with determination and said aloud. "Father is hungry. The hearty soup will warm him, although, first I must stoke up the fire, so we can have a cozy supper." Her voice broke, but she swallowed hard, and set her chin.

Rusty screen door hinges squeaked in protest and startled her. A familiar sound alive with memory, otherwise not noticed, brought comfort and warm memories, hidden in an indifferent heart, until now. Sarah's regular wood-gathering duties led her in and out of the same door, over and over again, in the winter, the squeak of the hinges a normal, acceptable sound. Each bedroom had a small fireplace, as well as the living room, parlor, and dining room. The cost of fuel necessitated the use of the raw lumber, and rooms remained closed off for conservation purposes. Ruth never thought about where it came from, or who supplied each room their fair share, only that it was always there, and the room was warm.

Wood splinters scratched through the thin sleeves of the cotton dress, but she ignored the small inconvenience. Inside Father's room, she started to heave the bundle, all at once, into the blackened maw that served as fireplace.

"No, child," Father admonished. "One at a time, no need to send sparks flying into the room. Let each one settle before you place another."

She dropped to her knees. "See Father, I am useless. I do not know how to perform the simplest tasks."

12

The last piece settled, the fire flickered higher, and the room brightened, bathed in soft amber rays. "But I will learn. You'll see. I will learn."

Before he could answer, she scurried down the stairs and into the kitchen. Two bowls of steaming soup, two slices of day old bread, and two cups of hot tea rattled on the tray as she ventured up the steps. At the top of the stairs, confusion stopped her. "I can't open the door." She looked around and smiled at the sight of the small table across the hall. "Sarah had this all figured out. Bless her."

Father beamed, watching her waltz into the room, platter balanced perfectly in both hands. Once all was arranged, the writing desk transformed into a table, and she relaxed.

"See, Father, I am not helpless after all. Just because I have never performed these tasks before, doesn't mean I can't do them. Now, tell me what you think of the soup."

He smiled and took a bite. "Ah, I declare, if I did not know you made it, I would think Sarah was back in the kitchen."

Both stopped in mid-bite. Ruth put down her spoon; a tear glistened in her eye.

Mr. Squire reached for her hand. "I'm sorry, daughter, I did not mean…"

Ruth shook her head. "Don't Father. I take it as a high compliment you would compare mine with Sarah's. She did teach me the art of making soup. Ever since I was a little girl, she forced me to watch on soup day. Her motto: If a woman can make a good soup, she is on her way to being a good cook."

"Sarah is one of a kind, that one. Don't think I didn't notice how the vegetables are sliced exactly as she would do it, at an angle. Her dishes were always pleasing to the eye, as well."

Silence settled like a cloak while the flames danced with a hollow merriment, and Ruth filled her thoughts with the next meal, and the next. How will I ever do it? Three meals each day, bread to bake, household accounts to settle, cleaning, tending Father…

He shook his head, added a spoonful of sugar to the tea, and stirred. "I know what you are thinking. We will hire someone, Ruthie. Don't fret yourself with the household details. I will be right as rain in a week or so, one less worry for you. Contact the agency and get someone over to interview. I know they can never replace our Sarah, but I will not have your hands cracked and reddened by cleaning, or your clothes ruined by carrying wood. You are going to be Peter's wife, not his servant. Besides, Mother will be home, soon."

She put her spoon down so hard the teacup rattled. "I will hear no more talk of Peter, Father. I am not going to marry him now, maybe never. My concern is for you, your health, this house…and…and… Mother. I can manage." She smiled and patted his hand. "After all, I am made of tough stock. Between you and Mother, I am strong as an ox."

He leaned back in his chair and sighed. "We will talk of Peter later. The warm soup hit the spot…and the fire has made me sleepy. I believe I need to lie down."

14

The tray of dirty dishes was removed to the hall. Ruth tucked a warm comforter up to his chin and smoothed the coverlet. Satisfied he rested comfortably; she gathered the dishes, ready to descend the stairs, when a knock on the front door interrupted her. Cleanup would have to wait.

The door opened to the constable standing, hat in hand, a half smile on his face. The middle-aged official was an old friend of the family. On this night, his otherwise cheery, plump face looked grim and tired. "Good evening, Ms. Squire. I hope my visit finds you well."

She opened the door wider and ushered him in. "Thank you, Officer Middleton, I am quite well. Please come into the parlor. Have you any news?" Too late, Ruth realized there was no fire in the receiving room, but it would have to do.

He twirled the hat between his fingers, anxious, jittery. "I do have news. Sarah has regained consciousness, but she isn't speaking, yet. The doctors feel it would help if you came to visit. The bullet grazed her head, and they conclude the trauma caused the coma. I hate to pressure you, but we need to find out the details of the murder. If Sarah could speak, well…"

Time stood still as Ruth absorbed the information. She paced to the door and turned back to the policeman. "Sarah is conscious. Then I need to see her, of course. Will you take me?"

"That is why they sent me. We can leave right away."

"What of Father? I cannot leave him alone."

15

Officer Middleton scratched his balding head. The next moment, a voice shouted from the front door. "Hey boss, should I keep the motor running or will you be staying awhile?"

A smile lit up Middleton's face. "Rogers can stay with him. We shouldn't be too long, and he couldn't be safer with a policeman watching him. How about it?"

Ruth shook her head. "Well, I don't know. What if he needed something, took a turn for the worse? It's pneumonia, you know."

"Rogers, come in here," Middleton shouted.

"Yes, sir, Constable, right away." The gangly policeman peeked into the room before entering, his long thin nose almost arriving before the rest of him.

The superior officer pulled Rogers into the room. "Do you think you can watch Ms. Squire's father for an hour or so while I take her to the hospital? He's got pneumonia, but is on the mend."

Ruth stepped between the two men. "No, no, I can't put him in the hands of a stranger. He's asleep upstairs… to awaken with a policeman in the house? Why, he would think something happened to me. The shock would be too much."

"You can go upstairs and see if he is still asleep. Maybe the racket we've made woke him. If he is awake, you can explain things to him. It's worth a try. Sarah needs you, too, Ruth." The constable gently touched her shoulder.

The younger officer spoke with a chuckle. "Ms. Squire, rest assured, I have had plenty of practice tending sick ones. We have seven children, and believe me, I take my turn plenty of times nursing them back to health. You needn't worry."

She looked from one to the other. "Well… if Father is awake. But if he isn't, I won't go. I do want to see Sarah, though. It's such good news."

Ruth walked half way up the stairs, stopped, looked back at the two officers, and smiled. "I'll be right back."

The door squeaked only slightly at her soft push. The room was darker now, the fire had burned low.

"Come in, daughter, and tell me what all the commotion is about downstairs." Father's voice boomed stronger.

"Oh, Father, you are awake." She rushed in. "Its good news. Sarah regained consciousness. She hasn't spoken yet, but the constable is here, and wants to take me to the hospital to see her…see if I can coax her to talk. They want to find out what happened. However, I don't want to leave you."

"Nonsense, girl, Sarah needs you. I will be fine. Just stoke up the fire and be on your way."

"There is a young officer here who volunteered to stay with you. Are you sure you don't mind?" The quilt slipped away from his chin, and she busily tucked it back.

He waved her away. "Stop fussing, Ruthie. You are wasting time. I will be just fine."

She whisked the tray off the hall table and hurried down the stairs. "He's awake, Constable. He has agreed I must go. Let me put these dishes away, stoke up the fire, and we can go."

Young officer Rogers stepped in front of her and took the tray from her hands. "I will take care of the fire and the dishes. Go on now, with the constable, and tend to Miss Sarah. We will be fine here."

Middleton held out her cloak, and Ruth chuckled as she slipped it on. "I sound like an old mother hen, don't I? Like my mother."

They rode in silence to the hospital, and Ruth reflected on the change overcoming her. *I do sound like Mother. Did I misjudge her all these years? Is her cranky demeanor the way she shows how much she cares? I never realized the burden she must have carried.*

Officer Middleton held her elbow lightly and guided her through the hallways to the room where Sarah lay.

A shiny stethoscope, shooting off shards of light, commanded Ruth's focus until they approached the door. It was then she realized it hung around the neck of a young doctor in a white lab-coat. She was afraid to see Sarah in that condition, and yet…knew she must. One minute Sarah was the sassy, finger wagging, bossy maid—the next she hovered close to death, maybe damaged severely. How could she look at her friend and know her own immature behavior was the cause?

The doctor put her at ease, at once. "Miss Squire, I am so pleased you decided to come. My name is Dr. Thornhill. I know how hard it must be for you. Sarah has worked for your family for many years, I am told."

"Is it horrible, Doctor? Will she ever be right, again? Can she even survive?" Ruth turned back to the hallway. "No, I've changed my mind. I can't do this."

The doctor stepped around to stop her. His gentle voice, almost lost in the cavernous hallway, was kind and calming. "Please, sit here, Miss Squire." He pointed to a long, gray bench against the wall. "Let me explain her condition."

A nurse bustled by, a food cart rattled past, and visitors wandered through one and two at a time. The physician ignored the distractions and looked only at Ruth. "The coma she suffered was not from an injury. We believe it was caused by emotional trauma. Yes, the bullet grazed her head, but it is a superficial wound and will heal nicely. If we can get her to speak, we will better be able to diagnose her recovery. We were hoping you would help us. She only stares, won't even try to make verbal contact. Maybe a familiar face will prompt her to speak. If not, it could mean temporary amnesia. I will tell you, she looks the same, no visible injury. There is a bandage on her head, of course. Won't you try?"

A glance at Officer Middleton, who nodded his agreement, and back to Dr. Thornhill, confirmed she was outnumbered. "Yes, after all, she tried to save Mother. Just this afternoon I tried to convince Father how strong I am. Now, I need to prove it."

The doctor's soft, brown eyes crinkled at the corners as he smiled. "I'll be there with you, Miss Squire. It's a very good decision you are making."

Her frame straightened, her chin lifted. "Please Doctor, call me Ruth. I am the head of this family now. I'm ready."

The room was dimly lit, and a curtain was drawn part way around Sarah's bed. A white gauze-like

19

bandage circled the blonde head, the only evidence of injury. Her eyes were closed. Ruth realized she had never seen Sarah asleep, never seen her lying down. Shame rushed over her. *Dear Sarah, I took so much for granted.*

The still hand was cool, but Ruth squeezed it gently. Sarah's eyes flew open. "Sarah, dear Sarah, it's me, Ruthie. Do you recognize me? You are going to be fine. It was a flesh wound, nothing serious. Can you hear me?"

Sarah's lips began to move, slightly. A moment later, a sound just under a whisper came from her mouth. "Ruthie?"

Ruth looked up at the doctor. "She spoke—said my name."

Thornhill smiled. "I knew it would happen. A familiar face is what she needed. Her recovery will be swift now."

Sarah's eyes twinkled. "Ruthie, it's really you." Her voice was raspy, but stronger. "Your mother...is she...?"

Once more, Ruth turned to the doctor.

He gave a slight shake of the head.

"Sarah, there is plenty of time for that, dear. Can you remember what happened?" Ruth squeezed the maid's hand, again. "It's important. Could you tell this nice officer?"

Middleton stepped closer to the bedside.

Sarah's eyes reflected instant fear. Her whispers grew louder. "No, no. Go away. He will kill me." A tear slid down her cheek.

No one means any harm, Sarah. You are safe, now." Ruth moved the officer back. "Later, you must come back later. Let her regain some strength. I promise I will help you, but she needs to rest."

Officer Middleton pulled Ruth aside. "I wish I could accommodate your wish, Miss Squire, but you see I can't. There has been a threat—a note, if you will. I fear your family is in danger, and we need to find the source. No one is safe, not you, not your father, especially Sarah. I have to talk to her now."

An Unlikely Beginning

Chapter Three

Four days earlier

Captain Alexander Adams, distinguished officer of the Navy, destined to come into a large fortune, rapscallion, and purported rapist, ran like the coward he was and didn't stop until he reached the pier. Oblivious to the strange looks and pointing fingers, he ran as if a ghost pursued him.

In a sense, the apparition of his youth did hound him. While his feet pounded the pavement, the past pummeled his mind. The ghost—Priscilla Squire, twenty years ago.

Beautiful Priscilla, seventeen, the belle of the ball. He had wanted her with such an ache in his loins those many years ago. Impetuous youth, callow numbskull. Vanity ruled him. Every girl swooned, each one vying for his attention. He had it all...the pick of the crop. The world lay at his feet, or so he thought. The dress she wore that fateful night burned in his memory. A deep rose color, abundant ruffles to set off her slim waist, creamy shoulders revealing flawless skin, glossy black hair. Never had he seen her dress in such a fashion. The new styles, to Alexander, were not flattering to a woman's figure, but this was a ball...formal dress was expected. She was the most beautiful girl there—and he wanted her.

Blessed with courtly good looks, Alexander Adams decided, early on, the world was created for him and him alone. His ramrod straight posture accented his height. Money, position, and a witty tongue made him the most sought after bachelor in town. Only he hadn't counted on the weakness of his own heart when it came to Miss Squire.

Their courtship progressed slowly, he wasn't anxious to cut ties with the other admirers, and Priscilla had her share of suitors. This night, however, his decision was made by the way she looked in that gown. He would ask for her hand.

The ballroom was crowded, the air stuffy, so he led her outside to the secluded garden. However, his plan went awry, and the unthinkable happened. All control was lost once he tasted those sweet lips, and he ravished her under the sycamore tree. He'd been oblivious to her cries of protest, her muffled screams. When it was over, she lay broken and crying in the garden bed, the rose dress in shreds. Like a coward, he ran. The risk to his reputation, the stature in the community, was too great. His father helped him join the Navy, where he carved out a career, married respectably, and spawned a daughter, Ella. But he was never to forget the night of the ball and the one woman he desired more than any other.

He stood at the pier, barely able to breathe, panting for air, remembering. The memory was too tortuous, too painful. The present situation slammed the past shut and forced him to concentrate. What just happened? His gun went off…Priscilla fell, blood staining her dress. Was it his bullet? There was a man—someone he didn't recognize, standing behind her. All he wanted to do was talk to her. Stupid idea to take the gun. *Was I afraid she would expose me after all these years? Once again, you acted stupidly, Alexander, but the worst of it is—you ran...proof you are the coward people whisper about as you walk by.*

The surroundings began to come into focus as he stood on the boardwalk. Logic told him to duck out of sight. Leaning against a doorway, a man in black stood watching him. Unable to move, he realized where he was, a seedy part of town. Over the doorway, where the man leaned, was a sign painted in blue letters. It read The Blue Feather.

An Unlikely Beginning

Chapter Four

Early Friday evening

Rivulets of rain wiggled their way down the window pane while tiny water droplets pinged on the gutters above beating out a haunting cadence. Peter watched the steady tracks of moisture, lost in the complexity of the design. The snow turned to rain, and the landscape became bleak like the foreboding in his soul. *I am losing her. Ruth is pulling away.*

A light touch on his shoulder returned the morose thoughts to the present. "Mother, I didn't hear you come in. You shouldn't be out in weather like this." He took the wet cloak and steered her toward the warm fireplace. "Sit down and warm yourself."

Elizabeth Kirby adjusted the damp hem of her soft, blue wool dress around properly crossed, slim ankles. "I went walking in the garden, dear, trying to make sense of all of this, waiting for the right time to tell you."

The chill in the parlor matched his mood, and the words she spoke took a moment to register in his distracted brain. He steadied himself, hung the cloak on the coatrack, all the while, hoping against hope she did not bear more bad news. One more wrong thing would be the end of his sanity. "Tell me, Mother? Tell me what? Did you overextend at the grocer?"

It was early evening; the younger brothers held vigil over their homework upstairs, supper was consumed…a perfectly normal day's end. So, why did he have a knot in his stomach in anticipation of the answer? He hoped for a flicker of a smile, but she didn't move.

"A visitor came today, Peter." She looked up, fear shining in her eyes.

The knot tightened in his gut. "What sort of a visitor. A man?"

A quiver danced on her bottom lip. "A very unsavory man."

Peter rushed across the room. "Did he hurt you?" It had been like a punch in his stomach when Father died. He'd spent the last two years protecting her from pain, building a safe haven around their family. The thought of anyone hurting her was unbearable.

"No, no, nothing like that. He left a letter—for you." Her hand fluttered to one sleeve and pulled out an envelope. "I didn't open it. After all that has happened…I was afraid."

He snatched the missive from her and stared at the unrecognizable handwriting. "Did he say anything, give his name?" A quick rip and the envelope was opened. He didn't hear his mother's answer. His heart skipped a beat…

We know who you are, Kirby. You killed one of ours, now it's our turn.

Peter's knees buckled. He sat hard onto the ottoman behind him and continued to focus on the note, hands trembling.

"Son, what does it say?" Elizabeth stood and moved close to Peter.

The parchment crumpled in his fist, reduced to a shriveled wad. "Nothing Mother, an unhappy customer, I fear. One of their bottles cracked on delivery. I'll have to replace the milk tomorrow on my route." *There is no way I will allow Mother to experience more uneasiness. In the morning, I'll take the letter to the sheriff.* "I noticed, yesterday, one wheel wobbled a bit. I'm going out to the barn and tighten the bolts. Can't have cracked bottles. No profit in that."

She stopped him in the doorway. "You shouldn't go out there, now, it's so cold and wet. You will catch your death." Her hand tightened on his arm. "Who was that man, Peter? He looked like a criminal."

For a brief moment, it occurred to him he should tell the truth. Prepare her, in case something should happen, but quickly dismissed the idea. "I won't have time in the morning, Mother. I'll need to replace Mrs. Austin's milk before I begin my regular route. I can't afford to displease another customer. The man was probably a messenger she hired. She's a widow, you know. Her children live far off. " He kissed the top of her head. "I won't be long."

Elizabeth protested, "But, why couldn't she have waited until the morning to…"

The words were cut off by the slam of the screen door.

Darkness hid the puddles, and more than once, cold water filled his sodden shoes. *I probably will catch pneumonia. What else can go wrong?* The warm smell of hay, mixed with dampness, greeted him inside the barn. Both horses whinnied softly at his arrival. Patch stomped his feet, while Bunny stood calmly beside him. Peter fished in a side pocket and found a couple of dried carrots, a standard treat he always carried for the team. The soft velvety nuzzles, while they nibbled the unexpected refreshment, soothed him temporarily. After the horses settled down, he plopped down on a bale of hay, drew out the crumpled letter, and stared at it, hoping to gain knowledge of the meaning. Nothing came to him. He examined the envelope and noticed something else inside. A blue feather.

How can anyone believe I killed the man? What is the meaning of a blue feather? Unwillingly, he bid the scene at Ruth's house that day to mind. Mrs. Squire lay sprawled on the floor in a pool of blood. Sarah looked unconscious, toppled across the bottom stairs, bleeding from her head, a pistol clutched in her fist. An unknown man fled out the front door. The real mystery was a man in a black suit, in the hallway, dead—half his head blown off. The police said he belonged to the mob. But why would he come after Mrs. Squire? Case of mistaken identity, maybe? He stuffed the note and the feather back in his pocket.

The safety of Mother and the boys was paramount. He had no choice but to take the letter to the police in the morning. *Maybe they can explain this nonsense. I didn't have a gun. Whoever wrote this note is mistaken. The only two people with guns in their hands were Sarah and the man who fled. I did see a gun in his hand didn't I? He's the one who must have shot the strange man and Sarah, but there were three people shot. Did he shoot Ruth's mother, too?*

The rain intensified. The racket on the barn roof disturbed the horses, made them restless; their feet shuffled, softly, in the stalls. *I know I should go inside,* *Mother worries so.* Once more, he pulled the note out, half expecting a magic answer to appear. None did.

A long, low rumble reverberated throughout the old barn, shaking timbers and stall doors. "The storm will be bad tonight. I best head to the house." The horses, settled for the night, would be fine; the barn, though a bit seasoned, was solid and would withstand the turbulence. It was the disturbance inside his soul that concerned him, an uneasiness growing with each passing hour.

Something didn't add up. The police missed something, a connection, or a clue. The note was a threat. Danger arrived at his very doorstep, today. Torn between protecting his family, and a need to reassure himself Ruth was safe, plagued him on the walk to the house.

"Mother, there is something I must confess."

The familiar clacking of knitting needles stopped. Elizabeth Kirby looked up from her work. "Confess? What could you possibly have to confess, Peter?"

His legs were planted apart, arms at his side. "The quiet of the barn gave me time to think. The note was not from an angry client…it was a threat. Someone thinks I killed one of the members of the mob—the man they found in the hallway behind Mrs. Squire."

"Son, you are dripping on the rug. Please dry off and come sit by me." The needles clattered their noisy rhythm, once more, in the quiet parlor.

"Did you not hear me, Mother? Not only am I in danger, but I fear you and the boys will somehow be involved. They know where we live. I…"

The needles stopped their chatter, and she stood. "I heard you and see how distraught you are. Admittedly, I too, was disconcerted about the unwelcome visit. Now I know the reason behind the intrusion, it seems we must use our levelheadedness to combat this misunderstanding. It isn't like you to lie to me, Son."

Laughter almost bubbled up inside him at the mention of his deception. In the face of the more serious matter, her ability to call him out on the lie while addressing the true problem was uncanny. "Mother, I cannot believe what the note said. Someone thinks I killed a man, and it's not the police! We could be in real danger. I am deeply sorry about the lie, but the way you reacted toward the events today convinced me I must."

While he explained, she retrieved a soft cloth from the drawer of the bureau and patted the sleeves of his jacket. Water ran off in tiny streams, the liquid disappearing in the braided rug. "We've weathered difficult times before. This is no different. At any rate, we cannot abandon our principles."

He grabbed her hand as it fluttered over his coat, and cupped her blonde head with the other hand. "The danger is real. I'm worried for your safety and the boys. You are avoiding reality again—like you did when Father died. Someone may want to hurt us. I can't let that happen."

A searing bolt of lightning lit up the sky, the crack of thunder rattled the windows, and Peter saw his mother's face in the stark light. Fear sat on her countenance like a stone mask. "I'm sorry, Mother. It is not my intention to frighten you." His arm went around her, and they moved together to the settee. "Sit, Mother, I will get some tea."

Another crack of thunder was accompanied by a pounding on the front door.

"Don't answer it," Elizabeth whispered. "It might be him."

Peter hesitated a moment. The second knock yielded a shout from the other side.

"Dang it, Peter. It's Deputy Randall, open the door. It's raining like the devil out here. I must speak to you."

An Unlikely Beginning

Chapter Five

The austere, unadorned hospital faced the city park; the window showcased a cluster of white pine in the clouded moonlight. Rain slid down the panes distorting the images, and lightening illuminated the twisted branches until they looked like arms with fingers pointing directly at Ruth.

She wrenched away from the window, stepped in between the officer and Sarah, and asked, "What do you mean we're in danger? By whom?"

The doctor stepped forward. "Now, Ruth, we were trying to…"

"No, him." She pointed to Officer Middleton shuffling from foot to foot. "He said we are in danger, and I want to hear it from him."

The constable, shoulders squared, steadied his feet, and cleared his throat. "We hoped the unpleasantness could be kept from you, Miss Ruth. The hard fact is with Sarah awake, your mother still in jeopardy, and Peter faced with protecting his family, well—it's time you knew."

At the mention of Peter's name, Ruth's heart pounded in her chest. "What of Peter, what has he to do with this?" Isn't it enough trouble has befallen my family, now The Kirby's are involved?

"The precinct has received two unsigned notes…we think they are from the mob. Both notes say they will wreak havoc if we don't turn Peter over to the Purple

Gang. A member of their mob was killed inside your home. Their biggest rival is the Kirby Gang, and since Peter's last name is Kirby, well—they're of the mind he did the deed." His forehead wrinkled, and he glanced at the doctor. "Don't you think she should sit down, Doc? We could have another incident on our hands."

She stamped her foot. "No, I don't want to sit down. Stop treating me as if I'll break. If we are in danger, it is your duty to inform me. The family is my responsibility, now."

A hoarse whisper came from the bed. "Ruthie, come, my child. I will tell you what I know."

Middleton nodded at Ruth, eyes expectant...eager.

The doctor, already at Sarah's side, tried to still her. "Miss O'Brien, you must remain quiet. You've had a nasty head injury." His hand pressed her shoulder. "Please, no sudden movement."

"Oh, whisht! I'm not knackered. Let me be. I want to talk to Ruthie." Sarah flung the young doctor's hand away.

Ruth's pure laughter echoed throughout the room. "She's speaking in Irish terms. I haven't heard those words in years. Doctor, you and Officer Middleton, leave the room. Sarah is right as rain. I'll find out what you need to know."

Officer Middleton protested, "Oh no, I'm not going any..."

"You'll go now, or I'll forbid Sarah to speak at all." Ruth walked to the door and opened it.

A stunned silence hung in the air, but after a moment, Dr. Thornhill grinned. "She's right, Officer. Sarah will tell what she knows—and the best thing to do, as I see it, is to let her tell Ruth. You do want the information, don't you?"

The policeman looked stunned, his mouth opened and closed, but no words escaped. Finally, a few nonsensical words tumbled out. "Well, I…that is…"

"Come on, the sooner she talks to Ruth, the sooner you will have the scoop." The doctor clapped one hand on Middleton's shoulder and gently pushed him toward the door.

The two women beamed at each other.

"Ruthie, my gal, it's good to see ya stand up for yourself. I'm that proud, ya know." Sarah's Irish brogue, stronger now, carried a hint of laughter.

"I learned it all from you, Miss O'Brien. Now, save your strength and get to the meat of the matter." Ruth straightened the bedcovers and handed the tiny maid a glass of water. "Whenever you are ready, dear one."

Sarah cleared her throat, attempted to sit straighter in the bed, but fell back, too weak to accomplish the task. "Well, here it tis, then. I knew something wasn't right that day." Her head jerked toward Ruth. "By the way, what day is it? How long have I been in this laudy daw place, anyway?"

"Just a few days, Sarah. Please, continue before they come back. We haven't much time, and their patience will run out." Ruth nudged Sarah's hand.

"Oh, to be sure. Well, here it tis, then. Your mum sat in the parlor, nervous as a cat, waiting for news of poor Ella." Sarah shook her head and clucked her tongue. "I was torn between my duties for dinner and the poorly look on Mrs. Squire's face. Truth be told, Ruthie, I decided to wait on the food to keep an eye on her. I just made up my mind and started down the hall when, from behind, a large, sweaty hand clamped over my mouth. It was that scared, I was."

The beat of Ruth's heart echoed in her ears as she listened to the story. "Did you see the man?"

Sarah shook her head. "Not at first. He pushed me down the hall with the pressure of a gun in my back. At least, I think it was a gun. Just when I thought I was a goner, a loud knock sounded at the front door. He pulled me behind the stairwell. Everything happened so fast, it's hard to recall...when he heard the male voice his hand dropped, and the gun went off."

Ruth's gasped. "Mother?"

Again, Sarah shook her head. "No, 'twas not your ma. He aimed for Cap'n Adams."

"Captain Adams? Alexander Adams? He was there—at the house?" The air returned to Ruth's lungs. "So the strange man didn't shoot Mother, Captain Adams did?"

Sarah whispered—eyes sad and full of tears. "It seems I am at fault for shooting your mother, Ruthie.

"You?" Ruth stood. "You couldn't have shot her. You didn't have a gun. What in blazes are you talking about?"

"Oh, be sure, I always carry a gun. A Derringer." A glint of a smile highlighted her face for a brief moment, but disappeared instantly.

Ruth lowered herself into the chair, once more. "I can hardly speak. All these years? I hadn't the slightest notion you carried a weapon. Did Mother know?"

"Yes, she knew. I have carried it since I left the homeland. My father gave it to me for protection. It was almost the first thing I showed the Squires when they hired me. I wonder where it is now, did the police take it?"

This time it was Ruth's turn to shake her head. "You know, I haven't heard anything about the weapons, or who shot who. Continue with the story, Sarah. How did you shoot Mother?"

Sarah glanced at the door.

"Don't worry; they won't come back until I summon them. Please go on," Ruth said.

Sarah gave a curt nod. "When the strange man dropped his hand from my mouth and moved to take a shot, I fished the gun from my apron pocket. Its funny Ruthie, I had never shot the thing before. Not in all these years…" A shudder wracked her shoulders. "It's then I fired the Derringer. Pointed it right at him— never hesitated."

"Okay, you shot him. How did Mother get shot?"

Her face turned toward Ruth, and tears welled again in her eyes. "When I shot… his gun went off. Reflex I guess. The bullet hit your ma."

Ruth stood again. "Sarah, you had no choice. If you hadn't shot him, he might have killed everyone. You can't blame yourself. I must tell the police." She started for the door, but turned around. "Wait. How did you get shot in the head?"

Sarah raised a hand to touch the bandage. "Cap'n Adams got off a shot before he ran. I remember the explosion close to my head. I guess it hit me."

Silence cloaked the room. The women extended the look between them, and Ruth imagined Sarah's unspoken thoughts. A millimeter…a mere fraction and Sarah could be dead.

"One more thing, Sarah. You said the strange man shot at Captain Adams. Did the bullet find its target? I believe you said Adams ran."

"I don't know, dearie. He might have been hit, but I couldn't tell. You see, I only had eyes for the man pointing a gun in the direction of your ma. Like I said, it was a matter of seconds, and then I blacked out." Sarah sighed deeply, exhausted. "I must rest. All this remembering has sapped my strength."

Ruth pulled the handle on the door. "You rest, Sarah. I will tell them your story. They won't bother you for a while. I'll get the doctor in here to look at you, first."

In the hallway, she looked around for the policeman, sure he wouldn't be far. At the end of the hall a cluster of blue uniforms blocked the entrance to the corridor. She spotted Officer Middleton. He saw her at the same time and motioned for her to stop.

The clip of his shoes echoed down the hall, a steady rhythm, yet for an inexplicable moment, the look in his eyes raised the hair on the back of her neck.

"Did she tell you what happened, Ruth?" he asked.

She heard him, but her attention was riveted on the object he held. He spoke again, his voice a sound of garbled words. All she could see was the plume he twirled between his fingers. A bright blue feather.

Chapter Six

A blast of cold air and pelting rain surrounded Officer Hubert Randall's blustery entrance before Peter could get a hand on the doorknob.

Peter met Randall a few years ago when the family first moved to Detroit. He was sitting on his front porch when Peter stopped to deliver the milk. The two struck up a conversation. The pleasant ritual stands to this day. The families share an occasional dinner, and Randall's wife Esther fell in love with Elizabeth's style and grace. The two became fast friends, a welcome blessing…a friend to coax her out of the doldrums.

"Officer Randall must you soak the carpet?" Elizabeth Kirby hurried to relieve the policeman of his overcoat.

"My apologies, but this wouldn't wait. Rest assured, I did not want to venture out in this weather and would have done anything to avoid it." He turned to Peter as he shook himself out of the dripping garment and allowed Elizabeth to hang it on the coat rack. "Might we talk in private, Peter? It's most urgent."

"Anything you have to say to me can be said in front of Mother. She is well aware of the situation. It does no good to hide things from her. It only serves to frighten her more." Peter motioned to the parlor.

Randall crossed in front of Peter at the invitation. "Suit yourself, you know her best, I suppose."

41

Elizabeth turned from the coat rack. "I've made some tea, if you will permit me to fetch it from the kitchen. It won't take a minute. Whatever it is you must tell us can wait five minutes." She didn't wait for an answer, but disappeared into the hall.

The policeman watched her leave. "She's a beautiful woman, that one. Anyway, while she's gone I can show you what we received in the mail at the precinct today." He fished around in his shirt pocket.

Before Peter could answer, Elizabeth reappeared in the doorway bearing a china tea service laden with biscuits and jam. "And what was it you received at the precinct, Officer? I believe I asked you to wait until I returned. Tea and biscuits?" She stood in front of the flustered man and lowered the tray to his reach.

Randall removed his hand from the pocket and gazed longingly at the inviting repast. "Oh my, that does look tasty."

Peter stood abruptly. "Mother, he said there is urgent business. We don't have time for refreshments. Now, what is in your pocket, Randall?"

The officer cleared his throat, stood, and drew out the item in question. "This, Peter."

"A blue feather? Another one? Is this a joke? What is the meaning of a blue feather? I don't have time for this nonsense. Either you tell me what is going on, or you can leave the way you came." Peter's irritation exploded.

"Now, hold your temper, Peter. It's no joke. We hoped you could tell us something. After all, the mob is after you, now. Do you have any recollection of a blue feather being tied to these crimes?" He waved the feather in Peter's face.

Peter drew a crumpled envelope out of his pocket. "I told you I did not. The only thing I can tell you is I received one too. Was there a note attached to yours…any explanation at all?" Peter asked.

"Nothing, only a second envelope addressed to Ruth Squire at the precinct address. One for you and one for her." Randall stuffed the feather back into his pocket.

Peter's heart leapt. "Ruth? Does she know, have you told her? I could not stand it if she was in danger."

The policemen reached for a biscuit. "Officer Middleton is with her at the hospital. He wants to show it to her…see if she can make any sense of it."

"Ruth is at the hospital?" Elizabeth grabbed Peter's arm. "Her father must have taken a turn for the worse. Or is it Sarah, or Mrs. Squire? Surely it isn't poor Ruth."

Peter slapped the biscuit from his friend's hand. "Out with it man! Why is Ruth at the hospital?"

The offended hand stayed poised in the air, while the officer's eyes widened. "Why, I thought you knew. Sarah regained consciousness. They thought if Ms. Squire came to talk to her, she would speak."

Peter collapsed on the ottoman. "I'm truly sorry, Randall. We didn't know. I'm very happy to know Sarah is on the mend. It's good news, indeed, but the feather? Or should I say feathers? What can they mean?"

Elizabeth began to spread jam on another biscuit. "Is Ruth in danger, also? What is all this nonsense about a blue feather?" She handed the jellied pastry to Randall.

The officer took the biscuit gingerly, but cast a furtive look at Peter. "We don't know, but Constable Middleton is worried you both might be in danger. The mob is nothing to fool with nowadays."

Once more Peter stood and walked toward the coatrack. "I'm going to the hospital. I must see if Ruth is safe." He turned to look at Randall. "Are you coming or is stuffing your face with baked goods part of your job, now?"

The biscuit disappeared inside the officer's mouth, after which, he swiped the back of one hand across his lips and grinned. "Doesn't do anyone any good if I faint dead away from hunger while hot on a case, Peter."

"I thought you said this was urgent." Peter kissed his mother and opened the door. "I'll be back, soon."

Officer Randall jumped up and followed him out. "Here, here, Peter. I'll drive you. No need in having an accident. You shouldn't drive when you are so upset."

"Fine, let's just go."

Elizabeth Kirby watched her son disappear into the squad car with Officer Randall through the window in the parlor, rain blurring the taillights as it sped down the road. "How I wish Ruth and Peter were married already. The union is meant to be, I know…but I also sense a foreboding. Can they be happy with so many people hurt?" She sighed and turned away. "Poor Mrs. Squire. I must pray that she survives this ordeal, as well as Sarah. It is all I can do at this point."

44

The stairway was dark now. She made her way carefully up to the other boys' bedroom. The rumblings on the other side of the door made her smile. *Homework must be done.* "Boys, it is time to wash and get ready for bed."

"Aw Mother, we were about to put the roof on the garage we built. Can't we finish?" Charlie implored with soulful eyes. The older of the two, he often took the lead in matters of convincing his mother.

Elizabeth shook her head. "Not tonight, Charlie. You and Joseph must do as I ask. The storm is pounding, I am tired, and I don't wish to have any arguments."

Joseph jumped up and ran to her, arms outstretched. "We would never do anything to upset you, Mother. We don't like to see you sad."

She held him close and sent thanks to heaven above for the love of her youngest sons. Life without a father took its toll on them, but Peter took on the role as head of the family, and Charlie and Joseph worshipped him. Three strong and healthy sons. They were her strength. "I am not sad, dears, only tired. Come now, say your prayers, and off to bed."

Charlie and Joseph knelt beside their bunks to recite the evening prayer. Both mentioned each member of the family and at the end, their departed father. It always gave her a twinge when she heard them speak of Robert, but knew it was her duty to keep him alive in their hearts.

Downstairs, she settled in the big overstuffed chair beside the fire, threw a quilt over her knees, and prepared to wait for Peter's return.

Peter and Randall approached the hospital desk at the same time, blurting out the question, "Where is Sarah O'Brien's room?"

"Well now, you cannot come bursting in here, loud and disruptive. I would have thought better of you, officer." The lady behind the desk clucked her tongue. "This is a hospital, after all."

Randall removed his police cap. "I am truly sorry, nurse. It's just that we have a matter of urgent business. I believe the constable is already with Miss O'Brien. If you could but point the way."

"Well...I suppose..." she began.

Peter leaned over the desk. "Miss, please. It could be a matter of life or death."

The nurse looked alarmed. "Third floor, room 308."

Both men nodded a thank you and ran for the stairs.

She called after them. "But mind you, be quiet. There are others in this hospital needing their rest."

Peter never thought three flights of stairs could take so long to climb.

The officer wheezed beside him. "Should have taken the blasted elevator."

"No time to wait for the operator. It's only three floors. Buck up, Randall." Even though he wasn't as winded as his buddy, he was breathing hard.

The door at the top of the third floor was closed, and Peter barreled his way through, Randall close behind. They stopped at the sight of several policemen in the middle of the hall. Ruth was a few feet away talking with Constable Middleton.

When she saw him her eyes lit up, and she closed the gap between them in short order, Middleton protesting behind her.

"I could not remain at home after I heard the news. The feather—do you know what it means?" Peter saw the glint of fear in her eyes, the tired lines surrounding them. He touched her face, lightly. "You look exhausted."

She placed a hand over his on her cheek. "Constable Middleton came to show it to me. How did you know about it? I haven't a clue what it means...wait, there is something. I only now remembered it."

"What are you talking about, Ruth?" Peter followed her gaze. The constable stood a step back holding the plume in one hand.

"Constable, the day my father and I came to the precinct—the officer at the desk, he told us where the shooting was...The Blue Feather Salon, on the dock. Could that be what it means?" She looked from the constable to Peter. "Remember? At the dock, the shooting happened right in front of a club called The Blue Feather."

Peter gasped, surprised. "You are right. In all the excitement, I forgot about it. So, it is the mob. I don't like where this is going."

Captain Middleton took a step toward Ruth. "We wondered if you would make the connection. The place is well known to us." He addressed Peter. "Son, I hate to do this, but we must take you into protective custody. You aren't safe as long as this gang thinks you killed their gunman. If you are behind bars, Ruth and her family will be safer until we figure this out."

"No! Peter…please, I don't understand. What have you to do with this mob?" Ruth rushed to stand in front of Peter.

His arms wrapped around her small frame to calm the trembling. "I have nothing to do with the mob, Ruthie. It's my name, Kirby. Because of that, they think I am a rival." Over Ruth's head he looked at the officer. "Unless you have evidence against me, Middleton, you have no grounds to lock me away. I run a business and am the sole provider for my mother and two brothers. I can take care of myself." He tightened his grip around Ruth. "I'm not going anywhere."

"Well, I am only trying to think about the safety of the public, Peter. We have so many murders in this town; I can't keep up with them. I don't want you on that list." He looked from Peter to Officer Randall who stood shaking his head at his boss.

"Who will protect my mother and my brothers while I'm locked away? What about Ruth and her father? I need to be free to care for my loved ones." The feel of Ruth in Peter's arms increased the anger, and the need to watch over those who were threatened. He knew he was outnumbered in this hallway, but the instinct to fight kicked in, and fight he would.

"There is no need for anger, Kirby. At second thought, it would be hard to protect your family out there in the country. I don't have enough officers to cover the town proper." He sighed. "I'll let it go for now, but if any more of these threats appear, all bets are off." His attention turned to Ruth. "Now, young lady, you need to tell me exactly what Sarah told you

48

Chapter Seven

Friday evening

Four days ago, Captain Alexander Adams regained cognizant memory in front of The Blue Feather Salon, a gun clutched in his hand. The man in the doorway had walked toward him.

"Gonna shoot somebody, mister?"

"What? No…I, that is…" Adams stumbled to explain the weapon dangling from his fingers.

The imposing guard reached down and pried the gun from Adams grip. "Not a good idea to come snoopin' around here armed. What business do ya have in this part of town? You don't look like no gangster to me? All those fancy duds." He fingered the braids on Adams uniform. "La Dee Dah. Ain't we all dressed up?"

Adams senses returned with the realization he was in deep trouble and alone. "I'm lost, that's all. Had something on my mind and wandered a bit too far. If you will give me back the gun, I'll be on my way." He reached for the weapon.

The man in black drew back. "Not so fast, Cap'n. You are a captain, aren't ya? I gotta a hunch about you. What's your name?"

Instinct insisted he not use his real name, but for whatever reason, his brain wouldn't function. "Adams, Captain Adams." Instantly, dread overpowered him, his heart beat in a rapid cadence, and perspiration beaded on his forehead. Stupid!

The gangster grabbed Adam's arm. "I thought so. You're the daddy to that little girl we snatched. What was her name? Ella...yeah, that's it. Pretty little thing."

A surge of anger replaced the fear. "You? My Ella was kidnapped by you? Why, I'll..."

Before Alexander knew what hit him, his arm was yanked behind his back in a painful hold. The air left his lungs, and he hung limp in the grip of the bigger man.

"So you come here for revenge, is that it? We'll see about that, Adam's. There's somebody you should meet. My boss will be mighty glad to see ya." He pushed the captain toward the door.

Inside the dimly lit speakeasy, Alexander tried to focus in the darkness. The club was obviously not open for business. Every corner of the room was filled with other gang members, some playing cards, other's drinking mugs of beer. Each one turned to stare at the spectacle the guard dragged through the main room. *This is bad; I'm in the middle of the gang that kidnapped my daughter.*

To make matters worse, the mobster decided it would be a good idea to announce this fact to the other occupants of the room. "Hey, looky here what I found out on the dock. A rat...a real live rat. Remember the little blonde dame we snatched from the school? Well, this here is her daddy. He's come to give us a piece of his mind, fellas."

Laughter erupted, chairs scraped, and several men came forward to size up the dandy dragged in by their main watchdog.

Adams squirmed in the firm grasp of his captor. "No, that isn't why I'm here. There was a shooting, that is…I shot…"

"Shut up, you sap. You gonna answer to 'The Nose'." He shook him hard. "I'd be sayin' my prayers if I were you."

The two men busted through the office door, Adams barely able to keep his feet under him.

A dark green, shaded desk lamp was the only light in the room. It sat on a wooden desk cluttered with papers, bottles of whiskey, and half smoked cigars — the air thick and sinister. Nothing good could come from this. Behind the desk sat a well-dressed man in a pin-striped suit and a black Homburg hat. A cigar glowed between his teeth.

"Whatcha got here, Moose? Some little muskrat snoopin' around? Kinda fancy dressed, ain't he?" Smoke rings floated into the air as he talked.

"I have here, boss, the very father of the little tomato we snatched from the school. The one that got Audie killed." Moose pushed Adams toward the desk. Thinks he wants revenge. Had this pistol in his hand standin' right outside the business. I nabbed him, quick."

The 'boss' put down his cigar and leaned forward. "Well, well, as I live and breathe. Now let me ask ya. Why you want revenge, mister? Your girl is safe and sound. No harm, no foul, I always say. Now it looks like you've got yourself in a peck of trouble."

Adams cleared his throat, raw with fear. "I didn't come down here for revenge." Moose gave a twist to the arm behind his back. "I didn't...you have to believe me. I know my Ella is safe. She is with her mother, no worse for the wear. You see, there was this woman...years ago. They called me from my duty station when Ella was snatch...er, kidnapped. I haven't been in town for years. The minute I stepped foot in town, the memories surfaced...I wanted to see Priscilla, that's all. I was stupid, I took a gun."

"You took a gun to see your lady fair?" The boss clucked his tongue. "Hardly romantic, Cap'n. Did you shoot her?" His ugly laughter filled the room.

All the air went out of Alexander. His head hung low. "I don't know. She was shot—not sure if I did it or not, too many other people..."

The 'boss' stood, his chair crashing against the back wall. "Wait a minute. You were at the Squire's shooting? You killed my gunman?"

Moose twisted the arm tighter.

Adams groaned. "No, I mean, I don't think so. My gun went off, but I'm not sure where the bullet went. There was Priscilla, a maid, and another man I didn't recognize. He shot at me. The gun discharged..."

"It had to be you, Adams. Somehow, I can't see Mrs. Squire or the maid wavin' a gun around. Do you know who I am, you bag of shells?"

Adams shook his head.

"Giovanni Zapelli. Most people call me 'The Nose'. I run this town, see? I just wanted you to know the name of the man that is gonna put a bullet in your head." Zapelli opened his desk drawer.

Moose interrupted. "Hey boss, maybe it's not such a good idea. Kirby was one thing, but this guy has money. It might bring the Feds down on us. We could use him, maybe. Be an inside guy. Just a thought, boss. Things haven't cooled down since Horton's body was found. We don't want more of 'em snooping around. I don't think this guy is the shooter. He's too stupid."

For the first time, Alexander saw a ray of hope. To save his skin? He'd snoop around all day long. He didn't look up, didn't dare to breathe—just waited for a reprieve. The room was silent, and for a moment, the thought crossed his mind that this goon had over-stepped his authority. Maybe 'The Nose' would shoot him, too.

He heard the slide of the drawer and the click as it shut. *I hope that means he changed his mind.*

"For once, you might have an idea worth thinkin' about Moose. I could use him to get on the inside. I want Kirby. He has to be tied to the Kirby gang. He's hiding behind that milk business. For all I know, he's runnin' the show."

While Moose and his boss talked about the plan, Adams wondered who this Kirby fellow was. He'd been gone a long time and couldn't recall anyone by that name, but if they wanted him to spy, he'd find out everything he could about him. Maybe, just maybe, he'd get out of this alive.

Three days passed. So far, an eight by eight room, with barred windows, on the second floor was all he had seen. One foot was chained to the iron bunk and his food was brought to him on a metal plate. He'd asked what the plan was...told them he was more than willing to co-operate, but the answer he received was 'the boss is checking into it'.

The window faced an alley, and he could see nothing outside of the small, gravel road running behind the speakeasy. The days went by in a monotonous cadence until Adams thought he would go mad. And then, when he thought the madness would overtake him, 'The Nose' came through the door.

"So Adams, I asked around. Your story checks out. It don't let you off the hook for shootin' my number one gun, though. You gotta make up for it, and I might let you live." The Nose walked over and fingered the chain around Alexander's leg. "I can't let you off of here without some sort of promise. Something to ensure me, you won't skip. Now, what do you think I might need as collateral? How about that pretty little daughter of yours? Bet she'd like to see me again. I'll take her out on the town. Introduce her to the more interesting side of life. Whaddya say to that, Cap'n?"

"No please, not Ella. Hasn't she been through enough? You can't take her again. The cops would nab you for sure if you tried it again." Adams stood and faced the jailor.

A burst of evil laughter filled the room. "As tempting as that is, Adams, I had a more interesting proposition in mind. She was quite a frisky dame, to be sure. The way I like 'em."

"If not Ella, then what...what?" He was eager to get on with the 'sentence', get this whole nasty business behind him, and leave this town.

'The Nose' put out his hand. "I'm thinkin' a little 'cabbage' crossin' my palm might change my mind."

Alexander stared at the man. "Change your mind? What is that supposed to mean?"

"I pretty much decided to 'ice' ya, Cappy. Moose here changed my mind. You see, I want Kirby, and I need to lay low since that stupid banker Horton ended up in a wooden kimono. That punk had something to do with my 'dropper' gettin' zotzed. I want revenge. Simple."

The room spun as Adams digested the information. Nothing registered except the part where he was to be killed.

"So, what's the answer, punk? You gonna work for me or are you gonna take a swim?" 'The Nose' tapped his foot on the dirty, wooden floor.

Alexander stammered, "Why would you kill me? I did nothing wrong. Lost…I told you I got lost."

"Look, you jingle-brained palooka, I said I was lettin' ya off the hook, but you have to do a job for me. You in or out?"

"I…I'm in. You want money, I'll get you money. What do I have to do?" Adams trembled, and it started to register. He was in deep, maybe too deep.

"Bring me Kirby. I want my pound of flesh."

Captain Alexander Adams nodded and sealed his fate. There would be no turning back now.

An Unlikely Beginning

Chapter Eight

Constable Middleton scribbled notes furiously, a low grunt accompanying each of Ruth's revelations as she recounted Sarah's story.

"So let me get this straight. This mug commandeered Sarah, but when a man came to the front door, he let her go—the mug fired at the man standing at the front door...Sarah shot the mug, the mug's gun missed the man and hit your mother. Is that about it?" He looked up from the notepad.

"Yes sir." She whispered, hoping he wouldn't ask any more questions. All that mattered now was everyone's safety. Peter waited in the hallway. She must get home. Besides, she didn't mention Captain Adams by name to the police and wouldn't. There was unfinished business with the scoundrel and it was her job to put it to rest.

"Does anyone know the identity of the man who came to the door? Can Sarah describe him? It's imperative we find him."

Ruth shook her head. "No, she was too frightened and focused only on the man in the hallway." You won't find him before I do, Constable. I have questions for the blackguard who sullied Mother's good name. He will do some explaining to me!

"Well, tomorrow I will talk with Sarah again. Maybe she will remember some scrap to help put a name to the stranger." He put the notebook in his pocket and stood.

Ruth's mind whirled trying to come up with a plan of action. I must warn Sarah not to mention Captain Adams to anyone.

The doctor stood outside the patient's door, waiting, even though the hour was late.

"Doctor Thornhill, may I say goodnight to Sarah?"

"Yes, of course, Ruth. Make it quick though. It's been an exhausting few hours for her." He smiled.

Though the room was dim, she saw Sarah's still form, eyes closed, as though asleep. Ruth approached softly. "Sarah, are you awake, dear?" she whispered.

"I'm awake, Ruthie. Was hopin' you'd say goodnight before you left. I want to know how your ma and pa are. Please tell me." She blinked against the dimness.

Ruth leaned down close to her ear. "Tomorrow, dear one. I will explain it all tomorrow. Right now, I have something urgent to tell you. Please don't mention Captain Adams to anyone. Don't describe him. As far as you know, you didn't see what he looked like. Can you do that for me? I want to find him before the police do."

"Now Ruthie…you're askin' me to lie to the pol…"

"Not lie Sarah, just not remember — yet. Please? I want to talk to the cad myself. I need to know why he brought a gun to our house. Promise me."

"I'm too tired to argue with ya, girl. Okay, for now, I don't remember what he looked like. Come tomorrow, then?"

Ruth planted a quick kiss on Sarah's cheek. "Yes, I'll come tomorrow. Good night."

Young Doctor Thornhill stopped her before she walked toward the others. "One more thing before you go, Ms. Squire. I think your mother is strong enough to withstand surgery now. I'd like to proceed in the morning, or in the next two days—with your permission, of course. The bullet could move. It's best we try to retrieve it now."

Weariness numbed her mind. *Not tonight, don't force me to make a decision tonight. Eric Horton's funeral, father's pneumonia, the blue feather, trying to keep Peter at a distance until I figure all this out. Please…it's too much.* She sighed deeply.

"Maybe you would like to talk to your father, first. If he is well enough, he can come and see her. The medication keeps her asleep. There's no pain, but she wouldn't be able to talk to him." The doctor lowered his voice. "Before we attempt to remove the bullet, I would want you both to see her, talk to her."

"You mean in case she dies? Be frank, Doctor. I have to know the truth."

He nodded, his face a mask of determination. "Okay…yes, it's a risky operation. She could die."

"I will talk to Father. If he's well enough, we'll come in the morning. I'll call you. Goodnight, Doctor Thornhill."

"Goodnight, Ms. Squire."

She stood silent, listening to his footsteps echo down the hall. Her body wouldn't co-operate, her limbs wouldn't respond to any commands. It was as if everything was disconnected.

"Officer Randall offered to see us home, Ruth." Peter whispered behind her. "I think we need to call it a day. Did you say your goodbyes to Sarah?"

His body drew her like a magnet, and without a second thought, she leaned against his strong frame, but drew back unwilling to yield. "Yes, but one more thing. I want to see Mother. If it's only to stand outside her room and look through the window. Can we wait one more minute?" The concern in his blue eyes warmed her. I could get used to leaning on him, but I mustn't. We have to untangle the mess I created.

"I'll walk you there." He called to Randall who propped himself against the wall, obviously weary. "Randall, we'll be a few minutes. Won't take long."

The officer gave a weak smile and touched one hand to his cap in acknowledgement.

Peter and Ruth walked to the room where Priscilla Squire lay unconscious. The strong presence of Peter's body striding next to Ruth, a strong hand under her elbow, provided a sense of assurance. Only Father had evoked the same sense of wellbeing. It was comfortable, steady…safe. But, she mustn't dwell on those thoughts. It made her weak.

The door to Mrs. Squire's room was blocked by a police guard, standing at attention, eyes straight ahead. Ruth was reassured by the sight. At least, Mother is safe.

Before Ruth could speak, Peter stepped forward. "This is Mrs. Squire's daughter. She would like a moment, alone. The doctor gave permission."

A surge of resentment coursed through her veins at Peter's presumption. The old, rebellious nature took over, and she snapped. "I can handle this, Peter. You need not speak for me." She stepped in front of Peter. "I'd like to see my mother."

Peter tensed, but stepped aside. A stab of remorse pierced through a self-inflicted imaginary barrier, but she steeled against the pain.

"I'm afraid I can't let you in, miss. The orders I have are no visitors, not even family." After a sharp nod, his gaze returned to whatever object favored his attention.

Cheeks flaming, Ruth was about to unleash a tirade against the unsuspecting policeman, but this time, Officer Randall eased his way around her.

"Jenkins, I have it straight from the doctor that Ms. Squire can see her ma. Step down, officer." He continued to block Ruth.

The hesitation was only momentary, and the guard moved aside so Ruth could pass.

A subdued Ruth looked at the man, said a whispered 'thank you', and pushed open the door. She stopped to thank Officer Randall, also, and disappeared inside.

The paleness of her face, the way she lay so still, wrenched Ruth's heart. One hand was exposed, and Ruth ventured to touch it. Surprisingly, the skin felt warm and filled her with hope. Maybe, just maybe... I have so much to tell her, so much I want to say. Please God... Out loud, she said, "Tomorrow, Mother. Father and I will be here, tomorrow. Rest, tomorrow will be a new day."

The stillness of her mother's body frightened her. This formidable woman, who ruled the household with an iron fist, now lay helpless and unresponsive —

completely vulnerable. Will I ever have the chance to make amends...to tell her I understand, now?

Naturally, there would not be an answer, not until tomorrow, and maybe not even then. She swiveled on her heel and walked to the door without looking back. *Mother would expect me to take care of Father, take her place, and do my duty to the family. I must not disappoint her.*

Peter and Officer Randall leaned against a wall, deep in conversation. The guard continued his vigil like a stone statue frozen in time.

"Peter, take me home. I must see to Father."

"Of course," he responded.

By his icy tone, she knew his pride was wounded. It couldn't be helped. She didn't know how or when, but she would tell him the marriage would not take place.

"Ruth, I want to talk to you. Please, let me come in, just for a short time? Besides, I want to see your father—pay my respects. Mother has asked after him, too. I dare not come home without laying eyes on him, myself." He took her hand. "I miss you. We haven't had a minute alone since that day at the dock." Peter held her hand as they walked to the Squire's front door.

"I am so tired—can we do it another time?" Ruth gently pulled away.

"No, we must talk tonight. My heart won't let it go another day." Pressing the matter was probably the wrong thing to do, but sleep would not come, tonight, without an answer.

The long sigh encouraged him. She would give in.

"I suppose for a few minutes. Father might well be asleep, though." Ruth unlocked the door and motioned for him to follow. "What of Officer Randall? Do you expect him to wait for you? The hour is late, Peter."

"I could take your automobile home. Mother could bring it back in the morning."

"I guess…"

Young Officer Rogers came striding down the hall, wiping his hands on a dishtowel. "Oh, you're back. I was cleaning up after a taste of your soup." He blushed. "Your father told me to go ahead and have some, since the hour was late."

"That's fine. How is he?" Ruth asked.

"Wide awake. I think he forced himself to wait up for you. You know, wanted to hear the news about Sarah." Rogers looked around. "Where is the Constable?"

Peter took Ruth's wrap and hung it on the coat rack. "He is right behind us. Had to finish some paperwork. Can we go up now, darling?"

"Yes, Peter. Officer, you can wait in the parlor for your boss. I see you put a fire in there." Ruth started up the stairs.

Peter allowed himself to relax. The fact Ruth let him in encouraged his soul. The yearning for her grew as each day passed. He wanted to feel her arms around him, her lips pressed to his. I will convince her to marry soon. I cannot wait any longer.

"Father, are you awake? I'm home. Peter is with me," Ruth called softly.

"Yes, daughter, do come in and tell me everything. Peter, it's so good of you to come." His voice sounded

63

tired, but joyful. There was no sign of coughing or congestion. "It is good to see you together."

"We cannot stay long. You need your rest." Ruth sat on the edge of the bed.

"Tell me the news, Ruthie. Did Sarah speak? What of your mother, did you see her?"

Peter walked to the window as Ruth related the news of Sarah and Mrs. Squire. *How can I convince her?*

The account of the events pleased the older man, but Ruth displayed no urgency to leave him to sleep.

He swallowed hard, turned from the window, but kept his voice neutral. "Mr. Squire, I fear I must ask you to pardon us. Ruth and I have details to discuss of the upcoming nuptials." It was bold, forthright, and maybe a deal breaker, but he had to take a chance.

"Of course, of course, you two go on. It pleases me to hear talk of the wedding. Mother will be delighted, as well." The mantle clock chimed the hour in the quiet room. "Ah, the lateness of the hour has rung out. I will finally see my Priscilla tomorrow, so go children, leave me to my dreams."

In the dimness of the hallway, Peter imagined he could see sparks shooting from Ruth's eyes. Instinct told him to nip the anger before it took hold. "Ruth, it's late and we need to talk. Get as mad as you want, but you will hear me out, first."

The only answer he received was the clacking of her heels down the wooden hallway.

Before she could descend the stairs, he grabbed her arm and pulled her back. "Wait. I want to talk...right now."

"Peter, I…"

"You aren't going to put me off, not this time. We are going to marry. You love me, and I love you. The shootings were not your fault. This has nothing to do with us. I won't let you slip through my fingers." The old house moaned in the silence after his declaration — ghostly sounds reflecting years of secrets and lies — hope and despair, life at its worst and best. He expected a protest and braced for it.

Chocolate brown eyes pooled with unshed tears stared up at him. "You are right, Peter. We will marry and soon. The sooner the better, I think. It will have to wait until after Mother's surgery, of course." She didn't pause, just took a breath, and continued. "Can we marry in the same church my parents wed? Would your mother mind? We need to discuss where we will live. Shall it be in town or out in the country?"

"Ruth, I won't take…" He stopped, stared at her, and then smiled. "Do you mean it?"

The clock on the mantle in the parlor chimed the hour. The warmth in his heart swelled as she caressed his hand with her cheek. "Yes, I mean it, Peter."

The touch was electric. The unexpected acquiescence made his heart soar. He wasn't going to lose her, she would, indeed, be his.

"But, Peter…"

"Yes, my love?"

"What of the blue feather?"

An Unlikely Beginning

Chapter Nine

Saturday morning

Alexander knew by now, his family missed him; maybe even alerted the law. Get Kirby. That's all he had to do. Bring the stupid lout to 'The Nose'. Should be easy enough. The hard part would be getting the money. Father had loads of it. The problem? The old man wouldn't let go. Lord knows, he'd tried all those years, but Father kept him on a meager allowance. It was plain embarrassing. "Me, a Captain in the Navy, and I must suffer the indignity of asking my father for money, even to support my family. He's never trusted me, never had any faith in me. Just because I made a mistake with Priscilla Squire twenty years ago. How long must I endure the personal affront of…"

The door crashed open, and Moose bounded in — practically tripping over his own feet. "Hey Cappy, good mornin' to ya. I got good news. You're gettin' sprung. Time to pay the piper, mate."

Adams jumped to his feet. "I'm getting out of here?"

"Hold on, bucko. It's you and me. Boss man says I can go with ya to round up old Kirby. Man, I can hardly wait. Sittin' around here is drivin' me nuts." Moose bent down to unlock the leg brace.

"You and me? Won't we look awfully conspicuous together? I mean, I'm a captain and you, well you…"

"Better watch your mouth, Cappy. Are you insultin' me? I clean up pretty good, ya know. At least, that's what the dames tell me." He leaned back and winked at Adams. "Besides, no one is gonna actually 'see' me. I'll be blendin' into the background—watchin' ya. Don't want you to get any funny ideas about skippin' town."

The nerve endings in his ankle twitched as the pressure released from the iron hackle. Exhilaration replaced the anxiousness as he realized he stood unfettered, but the realization hit him—the real work was about to begin.

The Moose clapped him on the back and pushed him toward the door. "Come on, the boss is waitin' on ya. You're one of us now. Have to get your instructions."

"You mean I have to follow a plan? I thought I might devise my own, you know, do it my way. I'm not a blood and guts kind of guy." Adams didn't like the feel of Moose's hand on his shoulder, but knew he dare not complain.

"Nah, 'The Nose' is the boss man. He plans every move. We ain't got a say."

Adams let Moose lead him out the door and downstairs to the office where they found 'The Nose' behind the desk tapping a pencil against the wooden surface of the enormous desk. "About time, Moose. What happened—forget how to use a key?"

The bodyguard pushed Adams forward. "No boss, sorry. Cappy here got a bit chatty. Askin' questions. I told him to speed it up, but he was draggin' his feet."

Adams stumbled toward the desk and stopped a foot away from the owner of The Blue Feather. Excitement turned to terror as he realized Moose had just thrown him under the bus. Hopefully, 'The Nose' would overlook his temporary lapse in judgment. Lesson learned. Don't trust Moose to have his back.

"That true, Adams? You been shootin' off your mouth?"

Adams shook his head vigorously. "No…no sir. I got excited, I guess. It's been three days; I was getting a little stir crazy. Remember, I'm a naval officer and used to being out on the high seas. I'm fine now, really. I apologize if I was out of line."

"Never mind that. You only get one chance Mister Naval Officer. You blow this and you'll find yourself under the water. Kapeesh?" The Nose opened a folder and pulled out a picture. "Here's your target. Peter Kirby, milkman, runs a route on the south side of town. Your job is to lure him here—to The Blue Feather." He pointed to his compatriot. "Moose here will shadow your every move. Try to duck out on me and it will only take one shot. Get my meaning?"

While his head bobbed up and down in agreement, Adams examined the picture. A blonde man and a dark-haired girl stood by a casket in the middle of an old cemetery. Uneasiness crept into his brain. "Who…whose funeral is this?"

"That's not your concern. Some stupid banker thought he was a big shot. Had to put him in his place. Turns out he liked to swim. How about you, Cap'n, you enjoy swimming? A big Naval Captain such as yourself?" The Nose reared back in his chair and laughed.

Adams decided not to answer the question, but asked another. "When do I start this job? The sooner the better if you ask me."

"That's better, Cappy." He turned to Moose. "Take him out in the main room. Have Fanny scratch up a meal for him. He's gonna need his strength."

"Aw, Boss, you know Fanny don't take to cookin' for strangers. I'll have to put up with her grumblin' mouth the whole time. Can't I just take him to the diner and feed him?"

"Can't take the chance of you two being seen together. Now, unless you want to join Cappy at the bottom of the river, do as I say." The Nose stood and pointed to the door. "Oh, and I want him alive. If you bring me a dead pigeon, it's the river for ya."

Moose grabbed Adams and shoved him out the open door. "Right, Boss. We'll make sure we don't ice him."

On the way to the kitchen, Adams wondered how they would execute this plan to abduct Kirby. The guy looked vaguely familiar, but he couldn't place where he'd seen him before, and the girl—he knew he'd seen her before.

True to Moose's statement, Fanny complained about the idea that she had to fix sandwiches for the two deadbeats the boss drug in. She moaned about being a star at The Blue Feather, and here she was reduced to a scullery maid. Her red sequin dress shimmered from the overhead light as she bounced back and forth gathering supplies. The scarlet fringe swayed angrily at her knees.

Moose and Adams muttered apologies under their breath, trying not to stir her displeasure even more. It did no good; however, as the tirade continued until she plunked two plates on the counter and ordered them to eat. With a resounding 'harumphh', she clacked out of the kitchen, fringe swaying and bracelets jangling.

"See what I mean, Cappy? Ya don't ever want to rile Fanny. You'll never hear the end of it. She sings in the club and thinks she's the star of the show." Moose took a huge bite of the sandwich.

Adams nibbled at his meal. "Does the Boss know she gets so upset?"

Moose nodded profusely and swallowed hard. "Oh yeah, he knows. I've heard tell he's slapped her around a few times, but he won't cut her loose."

"Why not, is she his girl?"

"Heck no. Fanny is his sister."

Adams looked up, mouth open. "Sister? Good grief, he slaps her around? What kind of jerk is he? His own sister…"

Moose laughed. "The kind of jerk who feeds guys like you to the fish. Slappin' his sister is child's play to him. Fanny and him…they grew up hard. She expects it when she gets out of line."

The rest of the meal was consumed in silence.

Adams watched Moose carry the dishes to the sink "Well, aren't you a good boy. Cleaning up after you eat. I'm impressed, Moose."

"You better do the same if you don't want to tangle with Fanny."

Adams carried his plate to the sink. He was in enough trouble; better not add another element to his situation.

Outside, Moose motioned him to a black automobile. "Get in."

As the hired gun sped down the road toward town, Adams asked. "So what am I supposed to do? Walk up to Kirby and say come with me? I find it hard to believe he'll come along without any trouble."

"We case him. Gotta follow him. See his habits, and then we spring on him. It might take a day or two."

Adams stared at Moose. "A couple of days? I thought we would get him today. I need to get home to my family."

"Not that easy, Cappy. We can't just take him off the street. We gotta be all subtle like. No one can know it's you and me doin' the abductin'."

As Moose expounded on the plan, Alexander Adams sunk lower in his seat. It isn't over. This may never be over. He was in the mob's clutches with no way out.

Chapter Ten

Saturday morning

Turmoil, gut wrenching turmoil! Ruth wanted to believe Peter when he said all would be well—the police would sort it out. At first, she resolved to put off the wedding, be a martyr, do the right thing, but how could she? The firmness of Peter's voice, the touch of his hands, melted any reservations. She couldn't live without him—not now. It didn't matter how much she wanted freedom, how strong-willed she had become. Through Mother's misguided parenting decisions, she found a partner, a man to trust...to love. The girl of seventeen had disappeared, and a determined woman evolved in her place. Maybe it was a bit of inherent stubbornness, or just a rebel nature, but here it was, exposed. Deep down, she unearthed the selfishness to pursue her own happiness, even though Mother might die and Father was ill. Should she suffer because of their ill-conceived idea of discipline? They wanted her to marry Peter, so marry him she would!

Father looked better this morning after a hearty breakfast. She managed not to burn the toast, and the eggs were sufficiently runny to suit him. The coffee was strong and hot. While preparing the morning meal, she dreamed the repast was for Peter. Her desire now? To be a good wife, a good cook. When Sarah came home, she would force those secret recipes out of her. *It's funny how a few weeks ago, cooking was the last thing I wanted to do.*

The dishes rattled in the sink as she forced Peter from her mind and began to pray for Mother, the upcoming surgery, and a miracle. Father brightened considerably knowing he would see his beloved today. She wiped her hands on the dish towel and looked at the clock...an hour before they must leave. There was one more thing to do. It must be now—before the operation.

The stairs appeared steeper as she climbed to the second landing, the hallway narrower. Each step caused an erratic charge in the rhythm of her heart. Finally, she stood in front of Mother's room and drew the key from the apron pocket. The violet fragrance, no doubt, would make it hard to enter, but she must. The key turned, the door opened, and she stepped inside. The scent, surprisingly, was light...evidence Mother had not been there for a while. Still, the shock overwhelmed her, and she almost turned to leave. No, I need to finish those letters. The truth must come out, and then, I will go after Captain Alexander Adams.

The closet door opened easily, mother's dresses hung stoically in front of her. She pushed past them, to the secret room. They were all there. The ball gowns, the jewelry, the innocent face of a girl twenty years ago—a girl Ruth did not know. Maybe the answer would be in the letters. She read a few of them before—knew Mother had found Adams attractive, and even wrote to him after the horrid incident. But why? Did she still harbor an attraction after what he did? The missing piece of that puzzle had to be found.

74

She pulled the drawer open. The letters sat neatly tied with ribbon, holding the secrets of a day long gone. She had only read the first three, finding it too painful to read the rest. The last letter found Priscilla almost begging for Adams to return and marry her. What was his response? She turned to the next letter in the stack.

My dear Priscilla,

I regret to inform you, I have been commissioned into the Navy. I have no recollection of the incident to which you refer. You must be mistaken. I congratulate you on your marriage to Robert Squire. He is a fortunate man, indeed. Wishing you much happiness,

Yours truly,
Captain Alexander Adams

"Cad!" Ruth slammed the letter onto the vanity. "What a coward. Poor Mother. She must have been devastated. To reject her like that, to deny it happened...why there might have been a child involved for all he knew. She inhaled sharply. A child? Could I...is it possible that I...

Father's voice called from across the hall. "Ruthie, don't you hear? Someone is at the door. Where are you child?"

The door? A hard, triple rap echoed up the stairs.

"Peter?" Ruth hurried from the closet, letters scattered on the floor. She stopped long enough to shut the door and turn the lock.

Voices called from outside as she dashed down the stairs and threw open the door.

Hattie Morgenstern and Cal Taylor stood side by side, beaming and breathless.

"Hattie, Cal, oh my goodness, it is so good to see you. Come in, come in. I'm afraid we can't visit long. Father and I are on our way to the hospital. Mother is stable enough for surgery, so the doctor says." The door opened wider, and the hall filled with chatter.

After all the pleasantries, Hattie blurted out the reason for their visit. "Ruth, we just heard. We couldn't wait to come and tell you how happy we are for you and Peter."

Shocked, Ruth allowed Hattie to crush her in a hug.

Cal patted her back, babbling his congratulations.

"What on earth are you talking about?" Ruth asked.

Hattie jumped back, grabbed Cal by the hand, and blurted, "Cal and I are business partners. We just signed the papers at the bank. We each own half interest in Mrs. Whitewood's Boarding House. What do you think of that?"

Ruth looked from Cal to Hattie. "Well, I...well, that's just wonderful! Business partners. Congratulations." A tentative hug was bestowed on each of her friends. "But what about Peter? You mentioned Peter and something about our good news."

"Oh, yes, I'm getting to that. I'm flushed with excitement about our new business. We wanted to tell the good news to Peter because I didn't want him to worry about me anymore." Hattie wagged a finger in the air. "You know...all that ugly business about the marriage betrothal and all. He's off the hook! Anyway, Cal knew where to find him on his route, so we drove by to tell him. That's when he told us of your plans to marry very soon."

Ruth stepped back and ushered them into the parlor. Strange palpitations hammered in her chest. "I didn't suppose we would tell anyone just yet, in light of Mother's surgery. We might well have to postpone it, you see…in case…if the surgery doesn't…"

Cal rushed over. "Now, I won't hear talk like that, Ruth. Your mother is a strong person. Besides, the doctors know what they are doing. Leave it in their hands. Have faith, believe. It will be alright."

"We are coming with you. It will help to have friends by your side." Hattie looked at her new partner. "Right, Cal?"

"I second that motion." Robert Squire stood in the doorway of the parlor. "The more support we have the better. Come, we must be on our way. I want to gaze on her face before they take her."

"I guess it's settled then. We'll all go together. I can't tell you what it means to have friends like you and Hattie, Cal. I knew you were true blue when I first met you at the boarding school."

Cal laughed. "Oh, no you didn't. You thought I was kidnapping you."

She smiled. "Well, yes, at first. Funny you should remember that. It was at your mother's house. I knew you were a person to count on. Thank you both."

The trip to the hospital was made mostly in silence, except for Ruth's father who chatted on about his beautiful Priscilla.

In the elevator, Hattie turned to Ruth. "Is Peter coming?"

"I didn't talk to him about it. There's the milk route to think about, so I don't think he will," Ruth answered. Secretly, she hoped he would make an appearance. Even with Hattie and Cal there, his strong arm of support would be comforting.

The elevator operator called the third floor, and through the iron grille, Ruth saw Peter in the hallway taking to the doctor, and a rush of pleasure surged through her.

Hattie and Cal saw him at the same instant. "He's here. Good for Peter," they cried.

Everyone crowded into the hall.

Ruth hurried to Peter's arms. "I am so glad you came, but what about your route?"

"You need not worry about my milk route, Ruth. I have friends in high places, so let's concentrate on your mother." He tightened the embrace.

The doctor touched Robert's arm lightly. "You can go in, Mr. Squire. She won't know you're there, but it will comfort you to see her. Come, follow me."

Robert smiled at Ruth and followed the doctor.

She watched them disappear down the hall, eyes misty, heart pounding. She must be alright...she simply must.

Hattie broke the silence. "Will you and Peter come to our grand opening, Ruth? Cal and I want you there. We're going to have a big party. I don't know many people here, and neither does Cal, but he's going to invite everyone from the boarding school. You and your parents know just about everyone in the whole town. It would be such good publicity."

Ruth smiled back at her friends. "Of course we will, Hattie. I'll make a list of people to invite."

Peter chimed in. "Did they tell you who is going to do the refreshments, Ruth? My mother. Isn't that grand? She will be so excited when I tell her."

Ruth laughed. "You haven't told her yet? What if she doesn't want to cook for that many?"

"We're talking about Mother, here, Ruth. She will take this project on as if the White House called for her talents. Finally, something she can sink her teeth into."

Cal cleared his throat. "I have an idea, if anyone is interested."

"Yes, Cal?" Ruth smiled. "Finally have something to say?"

"Don't be coy, Ruthie. I do have something to say. Why don't you and Peter get married at the boarding house? It has a beautiful garden area in the back. We could bring in flowers and decorations. If the weather doesn't cooperate, the grand parlor would make a perfect setting. Ruth could descend the spiral stair case. This could be the biggest social event of the year. A wedding and grand opening all at the same time. Think of it!"

No one spoke; they all looked at each other.

"Cal, that's a brilliant idea. I'm surprised I didn't think of it," Hattie said.

"I second the motion. A beautiful setting—all our friends and family. What could be better?" Peter agreed.

Ruth didn't speak. Emotion grabbed at her heart and tears trickled down.

Cal spoke softly, "Ruth, what did I say? I didn't mean to overstep. We've become such good friends, I only wanted to help."

Peter took her hand. "I think I know what is wrong, Cal. It's the church. Ruthie wants to marry where her parents were wed. Is that it, my dear?"

She nodded.

"I'll hear of no such thing, Peter. You two need to start fresh and new. That old church is too gloomy. I didn't even want to be married there."

Robert Squire stood in the doorway, beaming.

"But, Father…the church, it's a family tradition."

"Nonsense. It's dark and dreary. You and Peter need to start your life in a bright new way. I think your mother would feel the same way."

Ruth took his hand. "How does she look, Father?"

He smiled. "She is as beautiful as ever. You would never know there is a bullet lodged near her heart. I have a peace about this operation. She will be fine."

The doctor interrupted. "They are taking her up now. I will have my staff inform you of the progress. It may take a while. We need to take gentle care. All of you make yourselves comfortable in the waiting room."

They filed in, one at a time, and took their seats, silent, heads bowed as though deep in thought.

Ruth looked at each face. "Father is absolutely right. Our life should start fresh, in a new way, in a new place. Hattie and Cal, we accept your offer. We will wed in the garden."

Chapter Eleven

The tension eased as Alexander Adams and Moose sped toward the city. All he had to do was entice Kirby down to the wharf. *Surely they will let me go if I give them Kirby.* He let his thoughts wander to keep his mind from a more diabolical outcome. *Fanny Zapelli. Many years had passed since he laid eyes on a woman of her nature—worldly, a bit bawdy, mouthy, and extremely attractive.* "I always had an eye for the ladies. Father kept his foot on my neck, however. Said if I was ever caught with a woman of ill repute he would wash his hands of me. Instead, I've been forced to keep the company of those boring and proper women of 'breeding'. Nothing about any of them ever sparked a flicker of excitement. But, Fanny…now there was a real woman."

"What are you smilin' about, Cappy? Care to share the joke?" Moose punched Adams in the shoulder.

"I wasn't aware I was smiling. Nothing going through my mind, nothing for you to fret about. Tell me a bit more about Fanny, Moose. Does she have a beau?"

Moose glanced at him, sharply. "You got designs on her, Cappy? I gotta say, you like to live dangerous like. No one messes with the boss's sister. No, she ain't got no beau," he sneered. "Boss won't allow it. You better put the idea clear outta your head or you'll end up at the bottom of the river before this job ever gets started."

His heart beat a little faster. "The boss dictates whether she can have a boyfriend or not? He runs a tight ship."

"Don't tolerate no disloyalty, that's for sure. He ain't about to trust no guy with Fanny. Figures the bum will try to take over the whole operation."

Adams tried to push the memory of Fanny's backside prancing out the door from his mind. No time to be distracted now, with his life in the balance. Maybe, just maybe, later…

"There it is," Moose declared.

"What?" Adams looked up.

"Kirby's milk wagon. This is the end of his route. Now I wonder where the bloke got off to?"

Adams stared at the horses tied to the railing at the end of the block. A sense of reality swept over him. This guy is real. I might hold his life in my hands. He could die because I dared to show up at the Squire's. But they said he was a member of the Kirby gang. So why do I feel bad for him? I'm fighting for my own life.

"Okay, get out Cappy and tie this little present to one of the horse's bridles. We'll give him something to think about. Take care you don't let anyone see you. Make it quick."

"Me? Why me?"

"Because you belong in a neighborhood like this. I'd stand out like a sore thumb. Now do what I say, or do I tell the boss you got a hankerin' for Fanny?"

"Okay, okay. What is it I'm leaving on the horse?"

Moose handed him an envelope. "Take it out and tie it loose like on the bridle, so it's swinging in the breeze. It'll catch his eye real fast; put a little fear in him."

"A blue feather? Geesh, Moose, why doesn't the boss just tell everyone it's him threatening the town? You don't think the police will put two and two together?" Adams opened the door.

"The boss owns this town and the coppers. He don't much care if they know who's behind it or not. They can't pin nothin' on him."

Anxious, Adams looked around, closed the door, careful not to slam it. "I just hope the shooting doesn't start when I'm in the middle of it."

The horses whinnied at his approach, but stood quietly, like they were used to being tied to the railings. No one was about, nobody on their porches, or walking along the sidewalks. He tied the feather to the bridle of the biggest horse with the twine Moose gave him and walked briskly back to the automobile.

They eased away from the curb and drove toward town.

"Now what?" Adams asked.

"We find out where he went," Moose replied.

"How?"

"We've had a tail on him ever since the shooting. Shouldn't be hard to find out where he is. Gotta catch up with Stubby. He'll tell us."

Adams decided to keep quiet for the time being. Nothing about this whole operation sounded safe to him. Maybe the more he knew, the more dangerous it would become.

They stopped at a warehouse on the edge of town. Moose got out and knocked on the door beside the bay dock. A man opened the door, and Moose disappeared inside. Ten minutes later, Moose slid back behind the steering wheel.

"So?" Adams asked.

"He's at the hospital. Seems your precious Priscilla is having surgery to remove the bullet you put in her."

"I keep telling you, I didn't shoot anyone, especially not her. What is Kirby doing there?"

"The Squire's daughter is gonna marry the guy. He's up there for her."

His mind raced. This just keeps getting worse. Now I'm going to break Priscilla's daughter's heart to save my own skin? If I turn Kirby over to 'The Nose' he'll kill him for sure. I would give anything to change that day. Father is right; I'm the dumbest man on earth. I have to figure a way out of this.

"Moose, why do we have to do this? The men who are watching him—why can't one of them put a bullet in him? Why us, or more specifically me?"

"The boss ain't gonna kill him, Cappy. He's got bigger plans for Kirby. Gonna get him to run moonshine across the border." Moose laughed loudly. "Gettin' ol Kirby to work for him against his own gang...that'll start a war for sure. Should make for some excitin' fireworks."

"Is that all you people think about...killing and gang wars? What about common decency, families, homes—a solid life for the people you love." Adams shook his head.

"You're a fine one to talk, Adams. There's money to be made, that's all I'm thinkin' about. Now stop talkin'. We're headin' for the hospital."

An Unlikely Beginning

Chapter Twelve

At precisely 10:17 a.m. a matronly nurse appeared in the doorway. "The doctor will be in momentarily, the operation is over." The surgery lasted almost two hours. Robert stirred from the corner where he huddled, lips moving continually in silent prayer. Ruth watched the hope spring to his brown eyes and prayed the news was good.

She and the others had passed the time talking quietly of the upcoming events, each one offering ideas and advice, leaving Mr. Squire to his private thoughts. Now he rushed to Ruth's side to await the outcome.

The doctor entered and called Robert into the hall while Ruth watched anxiously at the animated conversation through the window. Peter held her hand and squeezed every few seconds. The pressure of his grip reassured her, kept her calm.

Mr. Squire returned, smiling. "Ruthie, she made it. It will take some time, but Mother will recover. He removed the bullet with no noticeable complications. We're going to get her back." More softly he repeated, "We're going to get her back."

Ruth collapsed into Peter's arms and rested in the comfort of his embrace.

After a few moments, Hattie tapped her gently on the shoulder. "Ruth, we're going now. We're so happy for you. I know you want to see her, so we will leave you to your family reunion. Let's get together in a few days to discuss the date of the wedding."

Ruth stood to hug her friends. "The two of you being here means the world to me. I can't thank you enough. I'll call you and let you know how Mother is doing."

"Ruthie, you should go home and rest. I'm going to stay awhile and sit with her," Robert directed.

"I can't leave you, Father. You aren't completely recovered."

Dr. Thornhill interjected, "Miss Squire, I think the best medicine for both of them is to be together. Mr. Squire is on the mend. It will enhance his recovery to be with his wife. We can put a cot in the room. He can rest there while he waits for her to awaken. If there is any problem, we'll call you."

Peter agreed. "I think it is a splendid idea. I need to get back to my route, so I can take you home. We'll come back after I've finished. You need rest, too, Ruth. Someone needs to care for your mother when she finally returns home. It will do her no good if you collapse from exhaustion."

Her shoulders relaxed. "Well...I suppose you are right. If everyone agrees, I guess I am defeated. Alright, I'll go home, for now." She started for the door, but stopped. "Doctor, what about Sarah? May I see her before I go?"

"Why, yes. Sarah is doing very well. I believe she can go home tomorrow. Her speech is good, and she seems to remember everything. It's a good sign. Why don't you stop by her room on the way out? She'll be glad to see you." The physician opened the door and stepped back.

"Thank you, doctor."

At Sarah's door, Ruth heard the familiar Irish brogue scolding one of the nurses. "Peter, she is at it again. I do believe the doctor is eager to be rid of her, sounds like she is running the place." Inside, she hurried to the maid's bedside. "Sarah, stop giving these nurses such a hard time. You're going home tomorrow. Leave them be."

"Och, and they call themselves nurses. They can't even tuck a proper corner. Why, I should…"

"I said you are going home tomorrow, dear. You can tuck all the proper corners you want. You'll be back to your old self in no time. There's good news, also. Mother's surgery went well. She'll need tending when we bring her home. So concentrate on getting better yourself. It's time you stopped lazing around here and do some actual work." Ruth grabbed Peter's hand. "We have more good news, too, but you will have to wait until you come home to hear it. That should give you incentive to hush up and get better."

Sarah sat up straight in the bed. "News, what news? You and Peter? Tell me, tell me."

"No, not until tomorrow. We'll see you then."

"I'll get you for this, Ruthie. You can be sure about that." Sarah shook her fist at them.

Peter and Ruth laughed and sailed out the door with a wave to the angry little maid.

The hallway bustled with visitors. Ruth followed Peter to the elevator full of good cheer and thankfulness. This had been a good day—the best in quite a while. She intended to enjoy it. The attendant asked which floor they needed and closed the door. Through the iron grill a shadow materialized and blocked the light filtering through the lacelike metal design. A voice, gruff and threatening, boomed. "Hold the door."

The operator's face registered apprehension, but slowly opened the barrier.

A man, over six feet tall, well-muscled, wearing a leather jacket and cap, pushed his way inside. Normally, the elevator held six people comfortably, but this man filled the entire space.

Peter circled his arms around Ruth in a protective manner and backed them both as far into the corner as they could get.

"First floor," he spat at the doorman.

"Yes, sir...that's where we're headed."

"I didn't ask for a blow by blow, mac. Just take me where I want to go." The stranger turned a menacing glare toward all three of them.

"No need to be rude, mister. The man is just doing his job," Peter said.

"Look, you pinhead. I didn't ask for your two cents worth. This is between me and the little flunky here. Keep out of it." He squared to face Peter.

Peter stood his ground and glared back.

The elevator stopped, and the frightened attendant rushed to open the door. "First floor, everyone out, please. First floor."

The man left the enclosure, but turned back to look at them. "If I were you, Kirby, I'd watch that mouth of yours. You never know who is listening." He disappeared into the crowded lobby.

Stunned, Ruth looked at Peter. "He knows your name. Who is he, Peter?"

"I don't know. I've never seen him before." He took her by the arm. "Come on, let's get out of here. It's probably some silly coincidence. Maybe he knows me from my milk route."

Perspiration dampened her palms...something was very wrong. Once again, reality overwhelmed her—the nightmare was not over. The memory of that day in the cemetery returned, the man behind the tree—but he wore a suit. This guy looked like a thug. Could they be tied together somehow? The mob? Whatever the connection was...the glow of the day dimmed.

Peter walked Ruth the few blocks to his milk wagon. Every shadow, every strange look from passersby made her jumpy. Would there ever be a day when things would return to normal?

"How about a ride home in style?" Peter asked.

"You mean the wagon—I suppose, but how will we get back to the hospital later? Our automobile is still there." Their steps synchronized in a pleasant rhythm, and in true gentleman style, Peter shortened his stride to accommodate her smaller ones. Funny, how in chaos, you notice the small things. There was comfort in the tempo, they moved as one with a single purpose.

"I'll telephone Mother to bring the auto. She would like to see you and your father. It's been hard on her to wait for news, alone, with no one but my brothers for company. Would you mind?" He hoisted her up to the seat before untying the horses.

91

She smiled down on him. "Why should I mind? I'd love to see Elizabeth. Have her bring the boys, also. I will prepare a little supper, and we can all go to the hospital afterward." Calm returned at the thought of a houseful of people again. She'd rest for a while and have plenty of time to prepare a meal.

Peter didn't answer, and she thought it took considerable time to undo the team. "Peter, are the horses alright?"

Peter was thankful the rope was tied on the other side of the wagon. The shock he was sure now registered on his face would only upset Ruth. The moment he reached for Bunny's bridle, the blue feather blocked out everything else— a blatant message. "Yes, they're alright, just tightening the bits. Be right there." I can't let her see this. She is only now calming down. He slipped it into the inside pocket of his jacket and climbed up beside her.

"You didn't answer me? Can you bring everyone, the boys, too? It will do me good to keep busy. We can talk about the wedding. Have you told her yet?" she asked.

The horses began a slow plodding pace down the road. Peter flicked the rein lightly. "Yes, yes, I can bring the boys, as well. I don't believe they have been to your house. They would probably enjoy it." He laughed. "Of course, they might do what they do best and destroy it. Are you prepared for that?" It would be good to keep them all together, until he figured out what to do about this second blue feather. I must talk to the constable again.

"Wonderful. I know exactly what to prepare. Certainly, I cannot compare to your mother's cooking, but maybe she can give me some tips. You know, I should invite Hattie and Cal. Yes, a little soiree in celebration."

"Whatever you wish, Ruth, please don't overdo, though."

"I need to be busy, Peter. Sarah will be home tomorrow, and I must get her room ready. She won't be strong enough to take over the tasks. I want to run the house. For the first time, I am excited about having a goal."

He smiled at the flush in her cheeks. This might be just the thing to keep her mind off the danger lurking over our shoulders. Let her have this glimmer of normalcy.

Ruth continued to talk about the little gathering, the menu, and the return of her mother and Sarah. It gave him time to think about a plan of action. He couldn't continue to allow these veiled threats to invade his family's everyday life. The situation needed to be resolved. Something dangerous was afoot and as head of the family; it was his job to take action.

"Peter, have you heard a word I've said?" Ruth nudged him.

"Every word, darling. I'm content with the sound of your voice. The happiness I hear is music to my ears," he replied.

"Oh, Peter, I can't tell when you are making fun of me or not."

"I would never make fun of you. The wrath that would ensue would be devastating to my physical well-being, my beauty."

"Peter, you are hopeless."

"Not hopeless, Ruth. Only a man in love."

Ruth laughed. "I must say, I haven't seen this side of you before. It's good to know you have a sense of humor. Most of the time you are so sensible and responsible."

His hand flew to cover his heart in a grand gesture, and he looked at her with eyebrows raised. "I have no recollection of the incident to which you refer, my sweet."

"What...what did you say?" she stammered.

The horses stopped at Peter's command, right in front of the Squire's residence.

"I said..."

"Get me down from her, at once."

Confused, Peter jumped down, turned, and reached for her. Once on the ground, she ran to the house, and he followed. "Ruth, what is the matter? What did I say?"

When she didn't stop, he continued pursuit into the house, and up the stairs. He found her in Mrs. Squire's bedroom, fumbling in a dress pocket hanging on a coat rack.

"Will you please tell me what it is I said to upset you?" he demanded.

Without a word, she unlocked the closet door and rushed inside. He had no choice but to follow.

It was not a pleasant experience to be back in this closet where so many hidden secrets were revealed, but obviously, something triggered a reaction in Ruth.

He turned the corner right behind her. She scooped up a collection of letters scattered on the floor, fingered through them, chose one from the middle, and shoved it in his face.

"This!"

An Unlikely Beginning

Chapter Thirteen

While his captor was gone, Alexander compressed his body as far down in the seat of the automobile as he could. Unwilling to be spotted by any casual acquaintance, he contemplated the possibility of escape. Why Moose trusted him to stay put was beyond him. Although, in some remote region of his imagination, he could hear the crack of a gun behind him as he ran out of the alley in which they sought shelter from prying eyes.

He didn't have to wait long for Moose to return.

"What happened?" he asked, sitting straighter in the seat.

"Don't open your trap until we blow this burg. Gotta enough to watch out for," Moose clipped.

Alexander noticed Moose pull his cap low over his eyes. It must have been something bad for Moose to be concerned about being seen.

Silence prevailed as they sped towards the docks. Once out of the city limits, Moose relaxed, pulled his cap back, and smiled at him. "You shoulda seen him, Cappy. I come face to face with Kirby—him and that little chickadee. Scared the bejeesus out of 'em both."

"What? You let them see you? I thought that was the whole reason you had me along, to throw off suspicion. Do you think it was a wise move?" He ventured a furtive look at the big driver. "What's the boss going to say when you tell him?"

Moose slapped his fist against the steering wheel. "We ain't gonna tell him, that's what. You breathe a word and you and your little scaly swimmin' buddies will be getting' reacquainted real soon."

All Adams could do was nod. He was in a fix. If he said nothing and 'The Nose' found out, he'd die. If he told…Moose would kill him.

"I gotta plan. Figured it out after I seen Kirby with his little tomato. She's a looker that one. Little mouse of a girl, though. Scared to death of me. Not my kinda woman, even though she's got the looks."

Adams waited for Moose to go on, but the big lug drove down the road with a sappy smile on his face.

"Get your mind off the dame, Moose, and concentrate on the plan. What is it?"

"Yeah, yeah. We get Kirby on his way home from his milk route. His habit is to check out the babe before he makes his way to the house where he lives with his ma. We nab him then. The girl won't be lookin' for him, and the mama will think he's with the broad. It'll be a long while before anybody misses him."

"What about his milk route the next day. They might miss him," Adams offered.

"By the time mornin' rolls around, we'll have him down at the docks, all tucked away nicely. Good plan, don't ya think?" Moose smiled at him.

"Hijack him from his milk wagon? You don't think someone will notice when the horses make a fuss?"

"We'll shoot 'em. They can't kick up a fuss then."

I wonder why 'The Nose' keeps him around? His brain is full of sawdust. Even I could come up with a better idea than that.

"Hey, what's your beef? You gotta better plan?" Moose's smile disappeared when he didn't respond to killing the horses.

Adams shook his head. "No, but maybe we better see what the boss has in mind."

"Aw, nobody ever likes my plans."

They arrived at the club with Moose still in a sour mood. Things didn't improve when they entered the dimly lit bar. 'The Nose' was leaning against the counter, cigar between his lips and a glass of whiskey in his fist. Adams knew right off word had gotten back to the boss about Moose's little indiscretion.

Moose hesitated, almost stumbled when he saw him. Adams stayed a distance behind.

"So, Moose. What the devil kept ya? Got somethin' you want to tell me?" 'The Nose' kept his gaze straight ahead and did not look at either man.

"No boss, I ain't got nothin' to tell ya. Got stuck in a little traffic is all."

"That right, Adams? Moose tellin' the truth?" Still, he stared straight ahead.

For the love of Pete, why did he have to drag me into this? If I say the wrong thing, we'll both be feeding the fish. "Moose, here, was casing out a plan, boss. He put a lot of thought into it, but in the end, decided it wasn't feasible."

The mob leader turned slowly toward both men. "You takin' over the operation, now, Moose. Is that it?"

"No, boss, it just came to me. Thought it might help get Kirby, but it's like Cappy said. It won't work."

"Suppose you tell me this plan of yours."

While Moose described the scheme, Adams prayed for a diversion. His prayers were answered.

"Giovanni, I'm bored. This place stinks. I gotta get some excitement in my life." A gum snapping, hip swaying, angry Fanny Zapelli entered the room from the kitchen. "You can't expect me to sit in this lousy dump every day with nothing to do and nobody to do it with." She pranced seductively over to Adams, fingered his collar, and chucked him under the chin. "What about the navy man? Can't he take me somewhere nice? I could get all gussied up; no one would ever know where I come from."

"Not now, Fanny. I got business."

She stamped her foot. "No, Giovanni. Now. You ain't puttin' me off no more. A girl gets lonely."

"Alright, alright. I'll see about the two of ya going to dinner someplace. Now will you leave me to my business?"

Fanny walked all the way around Adams, looking him up and down. "Yeah, he'll do just fine." The exaggerated swing of her hips made his heart pump. Not only did she just get them out of trouble, but he was actually going to go on a date with her. This could be the ticket to his freedom.

Meanwhile, Moose was getting a dressing down. 'The Nose' reached inside his jacket, pulled out a revolver, and twirled it on his fingers. "It's a stupid plan, you big goon. Leave the plannin' to me. I've been thinkin' how we're gonna do it."

"Sure, sure, boss. I'm an idiot. You're the brains of this outfit. Everyone knows that." Moose was visibly shaken.

Fear pierced Adams' heart as 'The Nose' turned to him. "So Fanny took a shine to you, eh? Don't get no ideas about my sister, see. She's bored, that's all. You're gonna get her unbored, but remember, I'll have a bird on ya every minute. Get out of line, he'll plug ya."

Adams stepped forward, one hand extended. "Look, I don't want to take your sister out. I have a wife and daughter. I need to be getting home to them. I thought we were going to nab this Kirby fellow, and then I could be on my way."

"Maybe you shoulda thought about that before you tried to rub out your lady friend. A thing like this takes plannin'. You ain't going nowhere, til I give the okay." The mob boss turned around and headed for his office.

He turned to Moose. "Now what? We just hang around here all day?"

Moose walked over to a table, pulled out a chair, and sank heavily into the flimsy contraption. "We wait. You might as well sit down. Nobody leaves til the boss gives the order."

He couldn't move, only stared at Moose. "This is what you do, hang out all day?"

"And drink. Pour me a whiskey, then get over here, and sit yourself down," Moose demanded.

Adams was used to being served, not acting as servant, but he obeyed. Behind the bar stood bottles of liquor by the dozens, lined up like little soldiers. He chose one, grabbed two glasses, and poured. Maybe he could make sense of all this with a little liquid fortitude.

101

Together, Moose and Adams sat across from each other and stared into their drinks, awaiting their orders…and possibly their fate.

The day dragged on, no activity, just booze and card games. His mind stopped functioning, a numbness settled in his brain. The light in the window started to fade, and one by one, members of the gang returned from their various assignments. No one spoke, and the only sound in the room was the scraping of chairs, and liquor being poured into empty glasses.

So this is what it's like to be in a mob gang. A lot of sitting around, waiting for the boss man to bark out the next hit. I'm part of it, now. I'm on the inside. God knows for how long, but I'm here now. The stories I've heard—no one gets out because they want out. Usually they end up on the bottom of the river. Will I ever get out?

Fanny Zapelli entered the room, looked at Adams, flounced over to the office door, and entered. Not even a knock on the door. Guys had been shot for less than that, but I guess if you are the sister to the boss, you can get away with it.

Fifteen minutes later, she emerged from the office, winked at Adams, and disappeared into the kitchen.

"Looks like you got a date with Fanny, Cappy," Moose announced.

"I hope not. As desirable as she is, it can only mean trouble. Besides, where could I take her where I won't be recognized?"

"The boss has it all figured, Cappy. Don't you fret none. He'll protect ya."

The office door opened, and Zapelli walked toward them.

"Take Fanny to the Golden Nugget for dinner. You can dance with her, but watch your hands. I gotta guy on ya. Get out of line and..." He squeezed the trigger on an imaginary gun. "Take him upstairs, Moose. Find him some rags to wear."

"Sure boss." Moose clapped him on the shoulder and pulled him to his feet.

As Moose shoved him up the stairs, he tried to ask questions. "I've never heard of this Golden Nugget. Where is it? How can you have clothes to fit me? Why can't I wear my uniform?"

"Shut up. You'll find out soon enough." Moose pushed him into the room, headed for the closet, and threw open the doors.

Inside was an array of suits, slacks, dress shirts, all manner of formal wear.

"Where did all this stuff come from, Moose?"

"Guys we rubbed out. Oughta be something in here you can wear." Moose rummaged through the hanging wardrobe.

Great, I'll be wearing dead man's clothes. I just hope there are no bullet holes in them.

Finally, with an obviously practiced hand, Moose selected the garb and handed it to Adams. "Get this on. I'll find the shoes."

He took the hanger from Moose gingerly, like he was holding a snake. "I have to put this on?"

"Yeah, don't worry. The goon wasn't killed in that one. We raided his house."

I guess I should be thankful for one piece of luck.

Dressed and groomed, Adams admired himself in the mirror. "Not bad, Moose. The fit is pretty good. Who was the guy?"

"Some city councilman who didn't want to go along with the boss's plan."

Reality spun back into focus, and the air in the room turned heavy. He really didn't want to know any more.

They went downstairs to wait for Fanny, but she was already there, dressed in a fancy red sequined gown, cut low in the back. Her head was adorned with the latest style hat with a red feather bouncing atop. She swirled around for their admiration, beads and bangles dancing in whispered tones.

The finishing touch…high heeled red velvet shoes.

Chapter Fourteen

Ruth thrust the letter at Peter. "How did you know Captain Adams wrote this to Mother? You repeated the exact same words."

He took the offensive epistle and scanned it quickly. "I've never seen this before, Ruth. I don't even know Adams. How could I? It's just an awkward coincidence. Surely, you don't think I've had any dealings with such an unsavory character as Captain Adams?"

She sank down on the vanity chair. "No, no. You repeated that phrase word for word. I was shocked, that's all. I'm sorry. Just when I think I've got all this handled, something makes it all come roaring back."

Peter knelt down beside her. "The world is a nasty place where people don't play fair and danger lurks around every corner. Here you are, in the middle of it. You've seen your mother and your maid almost die, your father devastated. It's to be expected. Time will lessen the anxiety, and I will be there to help you."

"I want to find him—punch him in the nose, ask him how he could abandon her underneath the tree, broken, bruised...disgraced." Her fist pounded the vanity. "I will find him. I will make him pay."

Peter pulled her up and circled his arms around her. "You will do no such thing. How can you run off to find a scoundrel when you have your mother and

105

Sarah coming home? Never mind a wedding to plan, a grand opening to arrange. What about all the invitations? Who will see to all that if you have run off, saber rattling?"

The smile increased despite her best efforts to remain distraught. "Oh, Peter, you do have a way with people. You make it sound as though everything is normal, as if planning our wedding was a well thought out plan. Do you realize how bizarre it all has become? Maybe we should postpone it. Really. Mother won't be up to it. She must be there. It is all her dream, after all."

His arms tightened around her waist, his lips found hers. After a long moment, she relaxed and gave in to the embrace. Gently, he pushed her back, turned, and maneuvered toward the closet door. "I am putting the announcement in the paper tomorrow; we will be married in a week. Your mother will be there, as will Sarah. No more argument, young lady." The door closed softly behind them. He took the key from her hand, locked the door, and dropped it in the house dress hanging on the coatrack. "Stay out of this closet."

The milk truck disappeared around the block leaving a desolate void in the house. The front door closed with a click, and she turned the lock. Rest was what she needed, but it would be difficult with Father at the hospital and Peter gone. "Not that I'm afraid. I can handle myself. It's just…I have never really been alone here. Sarah has always been about, even if Mother or Father weren't. So what? I can handle it."

The dark spot on the wood floor caught her eye. Bloodstains. She knew they had tried to clean it up after the shooting, but the stain was still visible, a grisly reminder. Peter was right, I need to put this all behind me and concentrate on the wedding. She hurried up the stairs to her room. A couple of hours of rest, and she'd be right as rain. There was a menu to plan, cooking to do. It would be a wonderful evening.

The bedsprings squawked in complaint as she lay down. Her eyes closed, but every creak of the house, every rustle of wind forced them open. This is silly. No one would come back here. They have no reason to hurt me. Besides, the police are surely watching this block after what happened. It would be foolish for someone to try to come into this house now.

Nonetheless, she sat up and locked the bedroom door. It didn't help. Now the house was too quiet. "Nonsense, I will simply think of the menu tonight. I can't have pot roast…that is what Elizabeth prepared for me. I must think of something different."

Two hours later, Ruth woke up refreshed, ready to tackle the small dinner party, excited to have something to do that resembled normal life. "I guess I finally fell asleep. Things always look different after a bit of rest."

Although the house continued the lonely silence, the fear had dissipated, and excitement took its place. She knew exactly what the menu would consist of and couldn't wait to get started. Peter would return soon with Elizabeth and the boys, and she wanted everything to be perfect. He offered to extend the invitation to Hattie and Cal, and she was glad it was one less thing for her to worry about. Soon, the house would reverberate with laughter and hope for the future. She rushed to the kitchen to prepare the meal and stopped dead in her tracks. One hand flew to her mouth to stop the imminent scream.

The outside door stood wide open, the screen unlatched, and a hole torn through the mesh

Peter, Elizabeth, and the two boys chattered away at the prospect of an evening at the Squire's as they motored down the country road toward town. Too long they had been forced to stay in the house, away from any danger, in hopes the criminals would be caught. Now in the safety of Peter's protection, good cheer prevailed.

"She's so excited to cook for you, Mother. I only hope she got some rest before tackling such a big meal. This is a first for her, you know." Peter couldn't be happier as he drove his family into town. The only dark cloud was the blue feather he still had in his pocket. That would be tackled in the morning, first thing.

"You can't imagine how thrilled we are to finally brave the outside world, Son. I know they haven't caught those men, yet, but one cannot stay cooped up forever. Anyway, we will all be together, and I am excited to hear of Hattie and Cal's news. Mark my words; I predict wedding bells for them, very soon." Elizabeth adjusted her dress and smoothed her hair.

Charlie and Joseph giggled in the back seat.

"Both of you hush," Elizabeth warned. "I will hear no giggling at dinner, tonight, either. You will behave like proper gentleman."

"Yes, ma'am," they chimed in unison.

"Now, Mother, don't go forcing your opinion on Cal. That's what started all of this remember? You and Mrs. Squire—matchmaking. Leave things as they are. They will find their way. It is a big step for them to partner in business.

"I'll know the minute I lay eyes on them. The love will beam from their eyes, and I will see it," she continued.

"Mother!"

"Alright, alright. I won't meddle, but mark my words…" She stopped to look at Peter. The automobile had slowed down.

Peter craned his neck as he approached the street. The Squire's front door stood open, and a policeman was talking to Ruth on the porch.

The roadster came to a stop, and in a brusque voice, he ordered the family to stay in the automobile. No one argued.

"What is it, officer? Ruth?" Peter came to Ruth's side, she was trembling.

"I went to sleep. Almost two hours. I woke ready to prepare for the party tonight. When I got to the kitchen, the back door stood open, a hole torn in the screen." She grabbed his hand. "Peter, someone broke in while I slept, went through the house, and left this."

He took the blue feather from her shaking hand, stared at it, trying to comprehend the meaning behind this new threat. "Where did you find it?"

"On the dining table. That is where the meal was to be served. How did they know? Was it a warning?"

At this point, the officer broke in. "Look, you can't stay here. Not tonight anyway. We need to search the place, see if they took anything, left any clues. Do you have a place you can go?"

"Oh no, I can't leave. Sarah is coming home tomorrow. Mother will soon follow. I need to get things ready."

A staccato honking came from the street. Cal was behind the wheel with Hattie waving from the passenger's seat. "Hello, the house!" They cried merrily.

Peter left Ruth in the company of his mother and hurried to intercept them. "Cal, Hattie, I'm afraid there has been a break in. It happened while Ruth was napping. Bottom line is she can't stay here tonight. The police need to investigate, and they don't feel it's safe for them to stay here tonight. The party is off, I'm afraid. I know you came all this way, but…"

Hattie interrupted, "They will stay with us, of course—at the boarding house. There is plenty of room. It's a week day so we have only one guest at the moment. I can get cook to stir up something in the kitchen, and we can talk about our plans. Ruthie wasn't hurt was she?"

Peter shook his head. "No, she was asleep when it happened. Found the door standing open when she went down to start the meal. She's very nervous right now."

"Then, it's settled. I won't take no for an answer. All of you will come for dinner. Why don't you go to the hospital and pick up Mr. Squire. By the time you get back, dinner will be ready." Hattie nodded at Cal. "That is if you approve."

"An absolute smashing idea, Hattie. I am looking forward to showing Ruth and Peter our plans for the place. Think of it—me a business owner." Cal grinned.

Peter hesitated. "Well, I suppose."

Hattie jumped out of the vehicle. "I'll tell her. She can't refuse me. Don't worry."

The two men watched as Hattie bounded up the stairs, took Ruth's hand, and talked in a very animated style. Ruth nodded, and the group made their way down the steps.

"Elizabeth and the boys are coming with me and Cal. Peter, you and Ruth will go to the hospital and fetch Mr. Squire. So get on with it," Hattie ordered.

The policeman had followed them. "We'll lock up when we are finished. I'm glad everyone has a place to go. We'll contact you tomorrow with our investigation." He headed back to the house.

The color returned to Ruth's face, and a hint of a smile played on her lips. "I was so looking forward to cooking tonight. You all must think I am a big baby."

Elizabeth hugged her. "Nonsense, child. No one expects you to stay here tonight after what happened. Hattie and Cal have come to our rescue, and I for one, am looking forward to seeing the boarding house." She turned to Peter. "So, go on now."

The two boys and Elizabeth piled into the back of Cal's automobile, waved, and chugged down the street.

Peter ushered Ruth into the automobile. He was about to pull away from the curb when he spotted a black limousine parked at the corner of the block. The

111

driver was not visible, but an uneasy feeling crept over him. The sooner I get Ruth away from here, the better. He kept watch in the rear view mirror and apprehension eased, slightly, after a few blocks. The suspicious vehicle did not follow, and for the moment, he relaxed.

Chapter Fifteen

Saturday evening

Fanny sure had a way about her. Alexander allowed the so-called lady to lead him out the door and into a waiting limousine. He didn't know gangsters lived so well. Not that he was complaining. After being locked in an upstairs room for three days, a night on the town with a fancy dressed woman suited him fine. A good meal, interesting company—he could get used to this lifestyle.

The Golden Nugget wasn't far from the club, so he didn't expect too much in the way of class. Probably a dive—a gangsters hideout, filled with smoke and guys with guns. Nothing could be farther from the truth.

Fanny talked non-stop all the way to their destination. For some reason, he discerned she must be a captive, too. There wasn't a threat hanging over her head, but even so, she wasn't free to leave. It was hard to imagine what her life must be like.

Moose wasn't allowed on this trip. Some big lug he hadn't seen before was the driver — not very friendly.

A shadow loomed beside the window, and he realized the driver was out and opening the door for Fanny. If any thought of escape passed through his mind, it was squelched instantly.

"I'll be watchin', so don't try any funny stuff." The threat came from deep inside the driver's throat, and it had the desired effect. The large, ominous man fingered the gun he allowed Adams to see under his coat.

He swallowed hard and nodded.

"Oh pooh, Vincent. Leave Alexander alone. He ain't gonna try to skip on ya. Why should he? He's with a beautiful dame. What more could a guy ask for anyways?" She grabbed his hand, pulled Adams away from Vincent, and up the stairs.

Surprisingly, the establishment was well lit, tastefully designed, and exuded an elegant air that belied its external image. That was Adams' initial observation. The more he looked around, it was obvious this wasn't a place for the mainstay, bourgeois population of Detroit. The room looked like a mob convention—pinstriped suits, black ties, fedora hats. The telltale sign was the bulge underneath the jackets of most of the men. They were packing heat.

The women, on the other hand, dressed for color and flair. Feathers, sequins, beads, and bangles. Beautiful, laughing, sexy women hanging on the arm of every man in the room. They were loud and bawdy, not the type of women in the pompous and prim lodges he was forced to attend. He found it shocking, but strangely alluring. The best part...Fanny fit right in.

She pulled him toward a table, but the maitre'd gruffly suggested another area of the club. A pout clouded her face for a moment, and Adams thought she was going to make a scene, but the cloud lifted as she looked in the direction the bouncer pointed.

"Collette, honey!" she called.

The dark-haired woman dressed in red sequins turned at the sound of her name. "Fanny, is it really you?"

The two women rushed toward each other, and Adams was pulled along with no choice but to follow.

They were invited to sit down at the table of several rough looking characters. He was hoping they could have been alone, but soon came to realize, he was the vehicle for Fanny to get out around her friends.

Two men dressed in the accepted garb of prominent mobsters eyed him as they sat down.

"Who ya got here, Fanny? I didn't think 'The Nose' let you out with no punks. This one looks a little prissy to me." A wiry, cigar smoking thug looked Adams up and down.

Fanny sniffed. "The name is Alexander Adams, and he's a captain in the Navy. So keep your stupid remarks to yourself."

The other goon pointed a cigarette at him. "Hey, I heard talk of him. Ain't this the guy who's gonna put the touch on that Kirby guy?"

Alexander didn't like the direction this conversation was heading. "Fanny, can't we sit by the orchestra? I see an empty table."

"Ain't you the fancy talker? Callin' the band the orchestra. The answer is no, honey pie. Sittin' too close to the music gives little Fanny a headache," she whined.

Both gangsters pushed their chairs back and stood, hands reaching for their holsters.

The wiry one spoke first. "You got somethin' against sittin' at this table, pretty boy? You too good for the likes of us?"

The hair on the back of his neck stood straight, and both armpits became damp simultaneously. "No, no, it's just I didn't want to intrude. Figured you didn't want any extra company." Alexander sat down when the taller goon kicked a chair his way.

Fanny pushed her way between the two tough guys. "Look Buzz, you and Valentino here, lay off my date. He's with me, and I won't have you ruining my good time. You know Gionvanni doesn't let me out too much, so cool your heels."

"Yeah, yeah, I'll lay off, soon as this pretty man quits insultin' us." The wiry one Fanny called Buzz retreated to his chair.

Fanny's face relaxed from a pout to a smile. "That's better." She shook Adam's arm. "I want a drink. Get me a drink."

He motioned for the waiter. "Sure Fanny, what are you drinking?"

"Champagne, Alex baby. I only drink champagne."

The waiter took the orders and disappeared into the crowd. The band struck up a lively tune, and Fanny started to sway. He didn't know if he should dance with her or even ask. No one gave him any real instructions about his exact role, but he didn't have to wait long for Fanny to make her wishes known.

The drinks arrived, and she grabbed a glass of bubbly and swallowed it in one gulp. Then, she grabbed him. "We're gonna dance, Alex baby."

He reflected how glad he was the song was a fast tune and wouldn't require his arms to be around her, when abruptly, the music changed. It was a slow, rhythmic waltz, and his heart sunk. His suspicions were confirmed. She took full advantage of the intimate song to tempt him beyond what was fair. Between the liquor and the music, he knew it was going to be a long night.

An Unlikely Beginning

Chapter Sixteen

Saturday early evening

Robert Squire slept quietly in the cot beside the bed of his wife. Ruth smiled at the scene, reluctant to disturb them. She whispered to Peter, "Maybe we should come back later."

His eyes flew open. "Nonsense...I've been waiting to share the good news." He sat up, rumpled and obviously sleepy, but with eyes twinkling. "Mother woke up. She actually spoke to me. It's the best news in the world."

They rushed to the bed. "Father, it's wonderful. I was almost afraid to hope."

"With any luck, she can come home in a week's time," he continued.

Ruth dared a quick glance at Peter. "I can't wait to have her home. Did you know Sarah is coming home tomorrow?"

"Yes, I know. After Mother went back to sleep, I ventured down the hall to see her. She was giving the nurses a hard time." He laughed.

"That's our Sarah. You know she is on the mend when she orders the nurses around." Her hand reached for Peter's. "Father, we are going to Hattie and Cal's boarding house for dinner, tonight. Elizabeth and the boys are there, too."

"I thought you were cooking dinner, dear. Chicken out?"

Peter stepped forward. "Sir, there has been a little incident at your house. I'm afraid someone tried to break in while Ruth was asleep. The police felt it was better if you and Ruth spent the night somewhere else. Hattie and Cal offered their boarding house."

Mr. Squire went pale. "Ruthie, are you hurt? Did you see who it was? Oh my, I could not take it if something happened to you. I should have been there."

Ruth took his hand. "I'm fine, Father. You were at the place you should have been, at Mother's side."

He hung his head. "Oh, when is all this unpleasantness going to end?"

"Come, Father. Let's go on to the boarding house and have dinner. You will feel better after you've eaten."

"Please, don't leave me, Robert." Priscilla Squire's voice was weak, little more than a whisper.

"Mother, you're awake." Ruth bent over to kiss her on the forehead.

"Yes, but," she turned toward her husband and reached out a shaking hand. "I want him to stay with me."

Robert took her hand in both of his. "Of course, my love. I won't leave your side."

"But what will you eat? I don't want to leave you here all night," Ruth protested.

Robert stood. "The nurses will bring my dinner. I couldn't enjoy a meal if I could not be near my wife."

Peter touched her elbow. "I think it's best, Ruth. They need to be together. I'll speak to the policeman at the door."

"Alright, Father. I wouldn't dream of separating you two, now that you are together again. We'll talk tomorrow."

Ruth said her goodbyes and joined Peter in the hall in time to hear him talking softly to the guard. "What are you talking about?"

"I filled him in on what happened at the house and suggesting he be on the lookout for any suspicious characters. We can't be too careful. Why they would be after your parents, I can't imagine, but we have to take every possible precaution."

"You don't think they would come to the hospital, do you?" She thought of the unpleasant man in the elevator earlier.

He sighed. "I'm trying to proceed with caution. The more he knows, the easier it will be for him to spot trouble. I fear for your safety, so the protective nature kicks in, I guess. After Father died, I hovered over Mother, as well—a weakness of mine." His half-hearted smile did little to mask his concern.

"Don't worry, Mr. Kirby. I'm here for the night. The shift doesn't change until seven in the morning. I'll keep an eye on things for you." The policeman shook Peter's hand.

"Yes, yes, we're going. Thank you, officer." Together, they walked toward the elevator, but Peter turned back. "Say officer, you look very familiar. Do I know you?"

The police guard shook his head. "No sir, I don't believe I've seen you before."

Ruth thought she saw a hint of a smile on the young officer's face. He answered awfully quickly. Doubt filled her heart, distrust her mind. Conflicting emotions warred and swirled, painful, confusing, and frightening. The world was changing, nothing made sense. Where was her youthful, carefree life? Shadows of a former existence danced like an old movie in her head...vanity, selfishness, narcissism, traits of a child. In their place—new characteristics emerged... responsibility, empathy, and understanding. Unfortunately, more distasteful features surfaced. Fear, of course, but now, skepticism, suspicion. Ruth felt the old self melting away, and in its place, a stranger, someone she wasn't sure she would like.

Peter drove carefully through town toward the boarding house. Uneasiness kept him silent, giving one word answers to Ruth's questions. He knew she was trying to distract him, divert his thoughts from the strange exchange with the policeman, but it didn't work. Somewhere, sometime, he had seen the man before. Nothing came to mind, however, no point of reference, no familiar memory. Was he just paranoid— creating suspicion where none existed?

"Peter, you passed the boarding house. Didn't you see the sign?" Ruth pointed out the driver side window.

He glanced quickly at the pretty establishment as they skimmed down the road. "I guess my mind was elsewhere. Sorry…there is a little road up here where I can turn around."

"Where were you, Peter? It isn't like you to be so distracted."

For a moment, he concentrated on maneuvering the automobile in the right direction and thought how best to answer. "It's a lot to take in, Ruth. It's my responsibility to keep the family safe and, of course, you. The new threat gives me concern about your parents, and Sarah, once again. The police said they want me, because of the Kirby name. So why target you…unless it's to get to me? I can't put your family or mine, for that matter, in danger. I'm trying to think of a solution. I'll be talking to the constable tomorrow." He turned off the ignition. "Let's not talk about it tonight. Let's focus on happier things with the others. Agreed?"

"Yes. Oh look, Cal's on the porch. He must have seen us go by."

Peter came around to open her door and whispered, "Now remember, keep it light this evening."

"Lose your way, old boy?" Cal sauntered down the steps.

"Never mind me, what are you doing out here? I figured Hattie would have you helping in the kitchen," Peter answered.

"If Hattie had her way, I would be in there chopping and slicing, but your mother shooed me out. Said I was in the way. She took over the whole kitchen. I don't know who is more strong willed in there, Hattie or Elizabeth. Glad you made it. I'll have another ally." Cal laughed.

"Oh, now I feel bad. I was supposed to cook dinner tonight." She hurried in front of Peter. "I must get in there and help."

The screen door banged shut, and the two men were left alone on the front step.

"Where are the boys, Cal?" Peter looked into the parlor window.

"Hattie has them set up in the living room. They are playing a board game and complaining of hunger."

Peter smiled. "They are always hungry." He walked over and sat in one of the large wicker chairs. "Sit down for a minute, Cal. I need to talk to you about something."

Cal joined him. "I'm listening, Peter. Is it the Squire's?"

"They are fine. There is a guard outside the door. I'm a bit uneasy about all of this. So many have already been hurt, I've got to do something."

Cal stood and paced the length of the veranda. "I get the feeling you are hiding something."

"You would be right. After we left the hospital this afternoon, I found a blue feather tied to the horse collar. I didn't tell Ruth, and now, I'm glad I didn't." Peter stood and kicked the flowerpot near the steps, sending it careening into the yard. "Why don't they come out in the open, show themselves? All this blue feather cloak and dagger nonsense isn't getting us anywhere. Maybe I should carry myself down to The Blue Feather and confront them."

"Whoa there, buddy. You know you'd end up at the bottom of the river, like Eric Horton. They think you killed their gunman. It would be suicide to go down there. Have you talked to the police?" Cal started down the steps. "It's also suicide to mess with Mrs. Whitewood's flower pots."

"The last thing I'm worried about is a flower pot, and yes, I'm talking to the police, but they haven't done anything. Don't you see, Cal? My being here puts everyone in danger, even you." He followed Cal into the yard and picked up the broken container.

"The police received the feathers along with notes attached, right? Were there notes on the ones you and Ruth received?" Cal tried to salvage the hardy mums, but they were scattered everywhere.

"No, just the feathers." He handed Cal the pieces of broken pottery. "I'm going to talk to the constable in the morning. No one knows about the feather left on my horse, only the one at Ruth's house."

The screen door opened, and Hattie stood with a large serving spoon in her hand. "What are you two doing out here in the cold? Dinner is almost ready — and what did you do to that pot of mums?"

"It was my fault. I stumbled backwards," Peter confessed.

"Yeah, stumbled," Cal agreed.

"Well, come along. We'll deal with it later. I don't want dinner to get cold." Hattie went back into the house.

"Thanks for covering, Cal. I don't usually let my temper get the best of me."

"Glad to do it. I don't want to hear any more talk about you being the reason all this happened. You and Ruth are getting married and that's it." Cal shoved him up the stairs.

The evening passed pleasantly with talk of the wedding taking center stage. The women chattered excitedly about the plans, and Peter's brothers fell asleep on the sofa having stuffed themselves quite properly.

Peter and Cal glanced across the table at each other, knowing the light-hearted evening might be the last one, for a while, until the gang members were held accountable for the threats. At the end of the evening, Hattie insisted Elizabeth and the boys stay over, as well as Ruth, so they could continue their plans in the morning.

The camaraderie of the women warmed his heart. He knew with Cal there, they would be safe for the night. Peter's horses needed tending; milk route could not wait, so he took his leave. He kissed Ruth and asked Cal to follow him outside.

"Keep them all here tomorrow, for as long as possible. I have my route to run. After that, I'm going to the constable. I'll be back to pick them up after lunch. Do you think you can keep them entertained?" Peter instructed.

Cal shook his hand. "I'll take care of the home front."

The ride home was lonely. He wished Ruth by his side, couldn't wait until they were married and could have her under his own roof all the time. The night was crisp and cold, easy for him to stay awake and notice his surroundings. It was calm, and if one didn't know better, the reality of the gang warfare and underground crime didn't seem to exist.

As he neared the turnoff for the family home, headlights appeared in the rearview mirror. Peter tensed at once. The vehicle followed at a distance, but seemed to keep pace with whatever speed he chose. He was relieved he'd left Mother and the boys with Cal and Hattie. The little country road came into view, and Peter's knuckles turned white on the steering wheel. It looked as though he wouldn't be arriving home alone.

An Unlikely Beginning

Chapter Seventeen

Late Saturday Evening

Alexander Adams opened his eyes and realized the music had stopped a few moments ago. Fanny clung to him, swaying slowly. "Fanny, the music's over. Let's go back to the table."

"Aw, Alexander baby. I like dancin' with you," she slurred.

He whispered in her ear. "I thought you wanted to look like a real lady tonight, Fanny. Real ladies don't act like this. Come on. Let's show this crowd real class."

She looked up at him, eyes misty. "You care what I look like to all these people? I'm not another dame to you?"

"Of course I care, Fanny. You are in my company, and you are beautiful. Let's not mess that up by acting low class. Here take my arm." He gently leaned her away from him.

Her posture straightened, her eyes focused, and she took his arm as they walked back to the table.

The rest of the evening, he caught Fanny staring at him, sober and thoughtful. The waiter came by to refresh the drinks, but she refused. They danced a few more times, but she held the frame, and gazed into his eyes.

In between dances, Buzz and Valentino asked him questions about the impending kidnapping. It made him uncomfortable, as well as leery. Were these guys testing him? Would every word he said get back to the boss? Sometimes the two goons would talk among themselves. He overheard them plot how they would nab Kirby. The ideas thrown around made him squirm, and the realization that he was in the middle of organized crime began to seep in. There was a strong possibility he wouldn't come out of this alive.

The evening came to an end with the driver tapping him on the shoulder telling him it was time to leave. Fanny didn't argue, and that surprised him. All in all, it had been a pleasant enough outing. Buzz and Valentino left him alone. Fanny turned all soft and adorable. He truly enjoyed her company and couldn't wait to tell Moose how sweet Fanny had been.

When they walked back into the club, 'The Nose' was waiting for them at the bar. "My boys told me you were a real good boy tonight, Captain. You showed my sister a real good time. There will be a reward in it for ya. Now get some sleep, cause we got some planning' to do tomorrow."

Moose appeared and crooked a finger for him to follow him upstairs. He wished Fanny a good night, thanked her for the evening, and did as he was told.

Halfway to the stairs, Fanny rushed over, pecked him on the cheek, and softly whispered 'thank you' in his ear. He squeezed her hand.

Adams figured Moose got his nose out of joint because he didn't enjoy the night out with him and

Fanny. He never said a word, but when the door closed he heard the lock click into place. Still a prisoner.

Peter let out a long sigh when the headlights in his mirror passed out of sight. Maybe his imagination was playing tricks on him. After a quick check on the horses, he slipped into the house with a little caution. They broke into Ruth's house; he supposed they could break into his. He walked quickly through the small rooms, but saw no sign of blue feathers or forced entry. Tomorrow, he would make a trip to the police station.

The next morning Peter woke with a start. Light poured through the windows penetrating his eyelids. Sleep had found him rather fast last night. It felt odd not to have the sounds of Mother in the kitchen and the boys arguing over the last biscuit. The house had a different feel without them here.

The milk route went quickly, and with time to spare, he headed for home to get the roadster.

Constable Middleton greeted him warmly and led him into his office. "What brings you around today, Kirby? Come to turn yourself in? I still say you should let us put you in protective custody."

Peter sat down in the single wooden chair across from the desk. "No need for that, Constable. I can take care of myself. Besides, Ruth and I are getting married in a week, and I want all this unpleasantness over. What can you tell me about the investigation?" He pulled the blue feather out of his coat pocket. "I didn't tell you yesterday, about this one. Someone left it on my horse."

The officer reached out and took the feather. "I really think this is all a little scare tactic. The precinct hasn't received any more communication from them. They probably want to put the fear in you. Let's see what the next couple of days bring. Congratulations on the nuptials. She's a pretty gal. How's she fairing after the little upset yesterday?"

Peter stood. "You haven't even gone down there, have you? Why haven't you sent someone to ask around?" He shook his head. "Ruth is fine. Everyone stayed the night at a friend's house." He crossed his arms over his chest. "Now what more are you going to do?"

The constable pushed away from the desk, sighed deeply, and stood up slowly. "Ain't much we can do, Peter. There has been no visible threat. Yes, someone broke in to the Squire's, but nothing was disturbed or taken. Until we have more to go on, I'm afraid we are at a stalemate."

Peter turned on his heel, looked over his shoulder, and said with quiet fortitude, "Then I'll have to do something about it myself." He opened the door and marched out of the building.

On his way to the boarding house, he mulled over a few ideas. Maybe he and Cal could go down to the docks and ask around. He laughed. The tables were turned this time. He had been the reluctant one last time, and Cal had rushed head long into the fray at the docks. Would Cal be so willing this time?

Charlie and Joseph were on the front lawn tossing a ball around with Cal when he eased into the driveway.

Cal shooed the boys into the house, all the while shushing the whining as the boys complied.

"Did you see the police?" Cal asked.

"I did, but I'm afraid we're on our own. They won't even investigate. The constable told me nothing was taken or disturbed, so there wasn't much he could do."

The two men stood on the porch, silent.

Peter cleared his throat, shuffled his feet, and plucked a stem of ivy from the hanging basket under the eave. "I'm thinking about going down there myself. You in?" He looked at Cal.

"That's foolishness, Peter. You are about to marry Ruth. Why would you put yourself in danger, or her, for that matter?"

"Well, I can't just sit around and wait for something to happen. What kind of man would I be if I didn't try to protect the family?" He plopped down on the wicker chair and tossed the ivy into the yard.

"What kind of man would you be if you went and got yourself killed? Who would protect them, then?" Cal answered.

Peter started to protest, but the screen door opened, and Ruth came bounding out to greet him. "I thought I heard your voice, Peter. Is everything alright?"

He stood up and kissed her. "Yes, no problems. How are things here, ready to go get Sarah?"

"All ready. I can't wait to tell her the plans for the wedding."

Elizabeth and the two boys joined the others. "We'd like to stay awhile, Peter. Hattie has some very good ideas for the parties, and the boys are having so much fun." She leaned over and whispered. "The garden beds need sprucing up. Hattie plans to put them to work."

"Well, I suppose this once wouldn't hurt. We have only a week to plan." He pecked her on the cheek. "I'll come back before supper."

Conversation centered around the wedding on the way to the hospital. He was pleased to see Ruth concentrating on Sarah, her mother, and the upcoming wedding. Sarah would be home with Mr. Squire. In the morning, he and Ruth would go to town and obtain the marriage license. The rest of the time, the women would be putting together the dresses and decorations. The perfect distraction—he could do some investigative work on his own without suspicion from the family. Now, if he could only convince Cal.

Chapter Eighteen

One week later

The beautiful, fresh bouquet of white roses, stephanotis, and baby's breath lay on the floor in tatters, tears staining the satin ribbons, and wilting the lovely blooms. Ruth crumpled to the floor beside the discarded flowers. She knew it was too good to be true. It wasn't over…it would never be over.

The week passed so quickly, she let happiness invade her heart and soul. Mother was home and doing well, Sarah was her old bossy self and taking care of business. Hattie and Elizabeth planned the wedding right down to the last boutonnière. She let her guard down, allowed herself to be happy, trusted Peter when he said he loved her. The shootings, the murders, the constant threats faded to the background, replaced by her own selfishness, once again.

Stood up — left at the altar. Peter never showed. Panic engulfed her as she realized he wasn't the man she thought she knew. A coward, that's what he is, afraid of commitment. Why, he was no better than Alexander Adams. Emotions clashed within while Hattie tried to comfort her. Mother wept softly in her wheelchair, and Father paced on the veranda. Elizabeth stood at the front door staring at the road, as if to will her son to appear. The guests were respectfully quiet, but one by one, they took their departure, affirmation the wedding would not take place.

Only a handful of people remained, standing around, whispering when Cal returned and hurried toward Ruth.

"The horses are in the barn. It didn't look as though they were fed. He wasn't anywhere in the house. His good suit was hanging on the door, pressed and ready to go. A tie was draped on the chair." Cal looked at Hattie. "The automobile is gone."

"He's run out," Ruth muffled her sobs in the lace handkerchief Elizabeth had given her for 'something old'. "He couldn't go through with it."

Elizabeth turned abruptly. "My son would never run out on a commitment. Don't you dare say that again. He loves you, Ruth. Something dreadful has happened, I just know it."

Cal rushed to put an arm around her. "Now, now, Elizabeth, nothing has happened. We can't think the worst. Maybe the roadster broke down, a flat tire, or the engine had trouble. It could be any number of things." Again, he made eye contact with Hattie. "I'll look around, go to the police station. The rest of you stay here, in case he shows up."

"What are you not telling me, Cal?" Ruth stood and faced him. "You and Hattie keep exchanging looks. I may be distraught, but I'm not blind."

"Nothing, I've told you everything I know, Ruthie. It's...well, Hattie and I like to confer on things before we take a plan of action. It's become a habit, I guess."

Cal's mother, head mistress of Barkley's School for Women, stepped in and gave Ruth a quick hug.

"Come, dear. Let's go have a cup of tea and calm down. Cal and Hattie seem to have a handle on how to proceed. We should let someone not quite so overwrought decide how best to do things." Mrs. Taylor steered Ruth toward the kitchen. "It'll be like old times back at the school."

"No, I want to…" Ruth began.

Hattie cut her off. "Mrs. Taylor is right. Cal and I will discuss what to do next. You are in no shape to make a decision." She gave Ruth a little push toward the door.

Mrs. Taylor stopped and addressed Peter's mother. "Why don't you come along, Elizabeth? A spot of tea would do us all good. We'll find out what has happened soon enough. Peter needs to have us all at the ready, not undone and unable to function."

Elizabeth nodded and followed the two women into the kitchen.

Cal pulled Hattie out on the front porch. "I don't like it. Nothing has been touched. It looks like he was never there. I didn't see any automobiles parked on the side of the road. I drove up and down his route, but saw nothing. It's like he vanished into thin air."

Hattie took his hand. "Do you…do you suppose?" She stopped and held his gaze.

"You mean—the mob? I don't want to think about it. Surely, they didn't get him." He wrenched his hand from her grip and turned toward the road. "He could be dead…in a ditch somewhere, or worse, at the bottom of the river. If it's one of the gang, we may

137

never know what happened to him." His voice fell into a whisper.

"Well, we have to find him, that's all," Hattie stated.

"Find him? How?"

"You've been down there, before. Right down on the docks," she continued.

"The Blue Feather? Do you think I should go there?"

"No one knows you there, Cal. It's Peter they were after, not you. Maybe you could snoop around, overhear something."

"You've been sheltered too long, Hattie, lived in the old country all your life. Things don't work that way in the city. The gangs rule everything. I could be killed. No, there has to be another way."

Hattie slipped an arm through his, and spoke softly, "We have to find him, Cal. He might need our help. Could be, we are the only ones who care enough. Ruth is in no shape to do anything. Who else? Elizabeth? At least, go and talk to the police."

"You're right, of course, Hattie. This whole business is so unpleasant. I never dreamed when I met Ruth life would become so complicated." He enfolded her in an embrace. "I never would have found you, though. It's all worth it, if I have you."

"Shh, let's not let everyone know just yet." She pulled away. "We have to make sure Peter is alright. Agreed?"

His cap lay perched on the arm of a wicker chair. He snatched it and secured it on his head. "I'll go now. It's probably a good idea we keep where I'm going to ourselves, for now. I would hate to upset Ruthie and

Elizabeth anymore. Tell them I went back to his house to feed the horses."

Hattie pecked him on the cheek. "Don't worry; I'll take care of it."

Cal knew a visit to the police station would be a waste of time, but for Hattie's sake, he wanted to cover all the bases. The wheels in his brain turned rapidly. The precinct would be a pit stop, and even though scouring the docks wasn't the thing he wanted to do, he knew it had to be done. The memory of Peter's sacrifice for Captain Adams daughter, Ella, came to mind. Peter had been anxious to find Ruth, even though he knew she was safe, but a girl he didn't know was still in danger, kidnapped. Ruth had been the target, but Ella was at the wrong place at the wrong time—a case of mistaken identity. Peter made the heart-wrenching decision to follow Cal down to the docks to make sure Ella Adams was alive, putting common decency ahead of his own desire. Cal had a favor to pay back.

The weekend crew at the station was sparse at best. The front desk officer didn't look very interested when Cal explained the situation.

"How do you know he didn't just run out on her, get cold feet? I can't do nothin' til he's been missing for 24 hours." The officer barely looked up from the newspaper he was reading. "You can go to that desk over there and let the clerk file a report. That's the best I can do." He pointed with a pen to a middle-aged woman in the corner of the room.

Cal hesitated. It was a waste of time, he knew. In the end, they wouldn't really do anything, but on the off chance...

"Name?" The woman pulled out the necessary forms and poised her pen.

Fifteen minutes later, Cal left the precinct and headed toward the docks. The streets hummed with traffic, the fading afternoon making way for a busy Saturday night. The closer he got to the seedy side of town, the more cautious he became. Wouldn't do to stand out. He decided to do a drive by, give the place a once over and head home. Better to do this thing by the dark of night.

Several automobiles were parked along the street near The Blue Feather, but he didn't see any telltale signs of activity. He eased toward the docks. Nothing. No one about — no activity. It would liven up closer to midnight, he figured. Time to head back to the boarding house. On the turnaround, he scanned the old buildings and remembered, the day they found Ella, the man in the window and the glint of steel. Reflex forced him to look up, and a strange feeling of being watched washed over him. Imagination he determined.

Hattie met him on the porch.

"How's Ruthie? Any news?" he asked.

"She is lying down. I put a sleeping powder in her tea. Maybe we can figure this out before she wakes. Any luck on your end?"

"No. I did as you asked and went to the police. They had me fill out a police report. Said they couldn't do anything for 24 hours. After I left there, I drove down to the docks. Nothing but a few automobiles parked here and there. I figure the real activity won't start until late at night. I'm thinking of easing down there come midnight."

"Could be dangerous, Cal. Maybe I should go with you." Hattie smiled.

"Real funny…no, I'm calling a couple of buddies of mine from the school. We'll ease down there on foot and see what's going on. I've heard The Purple Gang run booze across the border. Maybe I can see something."

"You will do no such thing, Cal Taylor." Mrs. Taylor stood in the doorway, hands on her hips, eyes flashing.

An Unlikely Beginning

Chapter Nineteen

"Hey, go easy with the cargo, Mac. The boss don't want no marks on him." Moose watched Mac and Adams drag the blindfolded Peter Kirby into the back room.

"Should we tie him in a chair, til 'The Nose' gets back?" Mac grunted, struggling with the weight.

Moose scratched his head. "Well, maybe…might be a good idea."

"I ain't got no rope," Mac answered.

"Then what did ya ask me for?" Moose jerked his head toward Adams. "Go find some rope."

Peter Kirby's head throbbed and bobbed loosely — all he could see were his shoes. *I feel like they slammed my head into a brick wall.* Bit by bit, he recounted the last hour, but the light pouring through the window directly in front of him hurt his eyes, so he closed them, and listened. Two men with limited vocabulary were discussing his fate. By all accounts, there was a third man, but he had exited the room. Something about a rope. Why was he here and what happened to his head? Instinct told him to remain still. As the fog in his brain lifted, he started to put the pieces together.

The week went by without any subsequent incidents. No blue feathers, no strange looking characters. Peter thought maybe the gangsters realized he was not who they thought he was and decided to drop the whole matter. His mistake. Excited about the wedding day, he started out the front door to feed the horses before heading on the morning milk route. A black automobile pulled into the driveway, and a well-dressed man, blond, with a wide smile, waved a friendly greeting.

"Peter! Peter Kirby, as I live and breathe." The man walked quickly toward him, hand outstretched.

"Good morning, sir. I'm afraid you have the advantage. Have we met before?" Peter hesitated before extending his hand.

The stranger shook Peter's hand vigorously. "No, no, we have never met, although, I feel like I've known you all my life. I'm a longtime friend of the Squire family. Why, I've know them since I was a young buck. Great people."

"Oh, so you are here for the wedding." Peter relaxed a bit. Even though there hadn't been any incidents, an alarm went off in his head. He intended to be very careful—especially, on this day. "You received an invitation, then?"

"Wedding? Oh yes, yes, I am here for the wedding."

"Why did you come all the way out here? The ceremony is on the other side of town. May I see your invitation?" Peter extended his hand, palm up.

The man patted his jacket. "Well, you see, I didn't bring it with me, didn't expect I'd need it. I came here on another matter. Business." He looked toward the house. "May we talk privately?"

"I have no business with you, Mr....what did you say your name was?"

The man reached into his coat pocket. "I didn't. But for your information, it's Adams. Captain Alexander Adams."

"Adams? *The* Captain Adams? I know all about you, sir. I want you off my property, immediately." Peter pointed to the auto.

"I think you will want to hear what I have to say, Mr. Kirby." His hand slid out of the pocket to reveal a pistol settled in his grip.

"So, you did shoot her." He forced his body to remain still. Father always told him to keep control of his emotion and maintain rational thought. One false move and his life might be over.

The gun wobbled in Adam's hand, and Peter saw the flinch.

Adam's struggle to sustain composure was obvious. "I did not shoot her. It wasn't me. There was another man in the house." Adams stood taller for an instant. "The man you shot, Kirby. It's all over town. You killed a member of the mob. I'd say that puts a pretty big target on your back—and your family, especially Ruth."

Peter took a step forward. "Keep my family and Ruth out of this. I'll deal with whatever comes my way, but my family is off limits."

"Hold on. I came to offer you a way out. Clear this whole mess up."

He shook his head. "I'm not going anywhere with you. The wedding is today. Besides, why should I trust you? You were there, I saw you run out with a gun in your hand. Everything you've said is lies."

"It won't take long, we have plenty of time. An hour at most. Come with me, tell your version. Give the man a little green, and things will be square." Adams smiled.

Peter moved slowly toward the front door.

Adams kept the barrel pointed at Peter and cocked the mechanism. "I wouldn't do that if I were you. I wanted this to be a nice friendly visit."

"How did you get mixed up in the mob, Adams? Did you sell out; need money, cross the wrong person?" Peter stopped, but kept an eye on the gun.

"Never mind about me. Are you coming peacefully, or do I have to shoot you in the arm?" Adams jabbed the pistol forward.

Peter laughed. "You must be crazy if you think, for one minute, I'd consider going with you."

The crunch of gravel startled him.

"I'm afraid you have no choice." Adams lowered the gun. "Meet my friends. They are here to make sure you play nice. You can get in the automobile quietly, or if you prefer, they can manhandle you until you comply."

Peter turned to see two huge thugs grinning from ear to ear. The larger one popped a fist into his hand. He knew there was no choice. "You win. I'll go, but I won't forget this, Adams. Rest assured, you will pay."

Adams didn't reply, only ushered him into the back seat in grandiose style.

Peter didn't believe Adams for a minute. The chances of getting out of this alive were slim, but logic dictated that he could die now, or at a time of his choosing. He preferred to play the odds and take his chances…for Ruth's sake, for Mother, and the boys. Between now and whatever was in store for him, maybe he'd find a way out.

The ride was uncomfortable. The two goons sat on each side of him, squeezing him in the middle. He could hardly breathe. Adams drove and chattered all the way about how much he had loved Priscilla, how he hadn't meant to hurt her, and how his father railroaded him out of town when he found out what happened. Peter didn't care about anything Adams babbled about. His mind was busy trying to figure out how to get out of this situation.

He began to recognize where they were taking him. Down to the docks, almost the exact place they had found Eric Horton's body. Before things got too familiar, one of the thugs pulled out a blindfold and tied it around Peter's head.

"What's this for?" he asked.

Adams answered brightly, as if they were going for a Sunday stroll. "Just a precaution, Kirby. The boss likes his private quarters kept secret. We'll take it off as soon as we are inside."

Private quarters? Peter thought. I have to try to figure out where I am. It's my only chance to survive.

They hustled him out of the car, and to Peter, it felt like they walked at least two blocks, turned one corner, and entered a building. They still didn't remove the blindfold.

Now, he was here, wherever 'here' was, with two goons standing over him.

"I think he might be about to pass out, Moose."

147

"Shut up, you pinhead. Don't use our names until the boss okay's it."

"Sorry, Moose."

Peter heard a slap and could only guess the one called Moose smacked the other one on the head.

"Maybe we should tie him in the chair. I don't know what time the boss gets back," Adams said.

"Good idea, go ahead, tie him up," Moose directed.

"I don't have any rope. We need rope."

"Well, go get some, stupid," Moose spat.

"Right—uh, where would I find rope?"

"Mac, take him to get the rope."

Peter heard another slap.

"Hey, what did you hit me for?" Moose hollered.

Mac's voice faded as he made his way to the door. "You said not to use our names, Moose. I figured that meant you, too."

"Get outta here," Moose clipped.

The door shut. Peter figured he was alone with Moose. He couldn't believe the low mentality of these guys. Even Adams didn't seem that bright. Maybe he could outsmart them.

Peter decided to try. "The boss got a name? Who am I going to be dealing with here, buddy?"

"I ain't your buddy, and I don't fall for no tricks, mister."

The door burst open, and Peter heard Adam's voice.

"Here's the rope, Moose."

Peter heard another slap, but kept his head down.

"Tie him up and keep your mouth shut. We'll just watch him til the boss gets here."

Adams mumbled something under his breath. The one called Moose jerked Adams away from Peter. "What did you say? You think I didn't hear that?"

In the ensuing struggle, the blindfold fell down past his nose, and he could see the room. "I didn't say anything." He quickly took in the contents of the room. It looked like a storage area. Boxes, crates, and beer bottles, broken chairs, and no curtains over the grimy windows. No view, either, just a brick wall outside. Must be the back of the building. An alley.

Moose was about to replace the blindfold when the door burst open.

"This him?" A man, dressed impeccably in a pinstripe suit, fedora hat, spats, and a cigar hanging out of his mouth sauntered through the doorway.

Moose nodded, Mac stepped to the back of the room, and Adams looked as though he would faint.

The room took on a completely different vibration, but Peter steadied his gaze on the object of the atmospheric shift. So far, he didn't see the big deal. The man didn't stand tall. In fact, he looked dwarfed next to Moose and Mac. He couldn't see how Adams stacked up, because he had retreated to the back part of the room. The only outstanding feature was the gangster's nose. The size of it more than made up for his lack of height.

"Why's he tied up?"

Moose stuttered and scrambled behind Peter. "Sorry, boss. I thought you might be afraid he'd get away." He fumbled with the knots binding Peter's wrists.

"Get away?" The boss walked all the way around the chair. "Mr. Kirby is our guest, Moose. He is free to leave any time he wants." He stopped in front of Peter. "I must apologize, Mr. Kirby. These two are not the brightest bulbs in the lamp. Let me introduce myself." In a swift motion, he removed his hat and gave a slight bow. "My name is Giovanni Zapelli, but everyone calls me 'The Nose'."

Peter remained silent, choosing to wait the man out...find out why they brought him here. The ropes slid off his wrists, and he brought his arms forward rubbing the sore spots.

"Ah, I see you are truly offended. I must remember to discipline the boys for their rough treatment of you." He pulled a chair in front of Peter and sat down. "Let me get right down to business, Peter. May I call you, Peter?" When he didn't answer, Zapelli continued. "I'll take your silence as agreement. Now, here's the deal. You took something from me, Kirby. All you have to do is pay it back. Complete the deal and we are square. Understand?"

Peter stood. "I have taken nothing from you, Zapelli. You have the wrong man. Now, if you will excuse me, I have a wedding to attend." He took a step toward the door.

Instantly, a metallic staccato resounded through the room as each hired gunman, including Adams, pointed a pistol in his direction.

Zapelli smiled up at Peter. "You won't be going anywhere, Kirby."

Chapter Twenty

Faded images danced in and out of Ruth's mind. She had a vague recollection of a glass of water floating dangerously close to her face, voices urging her to swallow. Blackness engulfed her, and the pain receded into its depths.

Now, there were no images, no voices. She was alone in the upstairs guest room. Objects came into focus. The dresser, pictures on the wall, the window— tree branches swaying in the slight breeze, scratching against the panes. The rhythm of her heart beat increased, and perspiration dampened her forehead. Memory returned, first in pieces, gathering together until the whole sordid picture filled her mind. Peter was gone. Walked out. Left her at the altar.

An involuntary moan escaped her lips, the pain rising to the surface in sharp, stabbing waves. The man she resisted—a marriage she fought against, now was the thing she wanted the most. All obstacles fell away; the painful transition from child to woman led her into the arms of a man she would love forever. Instead of a brass ring to grasp, a chasm of grief and betrayal stretched into the virtual unknown.

Her attempt to sit failed. Weakness forced her back against the pillow, and tears streamed down her cheeks. The will to try again did not exist.

A light knock on the door did little to revive her spirit.

"Ruthie?"

Hattie's voice registered in her brain—she turned toward the sound.

"Are you awake, dear? You've been asleep for hours. You need to eat…and we need to talk." Hattie swept into the room and walked to the window to push the curtains open.

Ruth groaned as the light assaulted her eyes. "If I've been asleep for hours, why is it still daylight?"

"Okay, three hours." Hattie sat hard on the bed and threw the coverlet off of Ruth. "Do you intend to sleep forever, or are you going to fight for the man you love?"

"He left me, remember, Miss Morgenstern? There is no fight."

"Nonsense, I don't believe it for a minute. Peter is a good person. Why, he is so in love with you he can hardly see straight. Something else has happened, and Cal is going to find out what." Hattie retrieved Ruth's shoes from under the bed and shoved them at her.

Ruth stood so quickly, the shoes flew across the room.

"What do you mean Cal is going to find out what happened? Do you know something more than you are telling me?" Ruth glanced around the room, found one shoe under the dresser, and retrieved it.

"He doesn't know anything, but we trust Peter. There is no note, he left his horses unattended. Ruth, I am surprised you can even doubt him." Hattie grabbed the other shoe from under the vanity chair and handed it to her.

"The past few months have been so bizarre. So many crazy things happening. I don't know what to believe, Hattie. Don't you think I want to trust and believe in him?" She started toward the door. "Take me to Cal. I want to talk to him."

"I can't. He's gone. Not sure when he will be back." Hattie started out the door. "I do know you need to eat. Come down to the kitchen."

Ruth followed, protesting. "Hattie Morgenstern, you tell me where Cal is this instant. If he has gone to look for him, I want to go along."

"Fat chance. Where Cal is going is no place for the likes of you."

At the bottom stair, Ruth heard the screen door slam. "Is that you, Cal?"

"No, Miss Ruth. It's me, Charlie." Peter's brothers scrambled toward the kitchen.

The sight of their blond heads made Ruth's heart leap. She grabbed Hattie's arm to steady herself. "Maybe I do need to eat. I can't look for Peter on an empty stomach."

The kitchen was the hub of all the activity in the house. Cook was stirring something in a large pot on the stove, the boys were peering into the refrigerator, Elizabeth tended the teapot, and even Ruth's mother was folding dishtowels in the corner. They all smiled in greeting as she entered.

"Look who is awake," Hattie announced.

"Good to see you got some rest, dear." Elizabeth smiled, but the creases around her eyes told the story of the stressful situation.

"Mother, you shouldn't be over doing, right now. You haven't been home very long. Let me do that." She started toward the wheelchair Priscilla occupied.

"Nonsense, girl. Folding towels is not an exertion. Besides, Hattie and Elizabeth have kept an eagle eye on me. I must try to make myself feel useful. After all…"

"Mother, I will hear none of that. Fine, I am a bit hungry. I'll make a sandwich — then, I can help the rest of you."

Cook turned and presented a plate with a fine turkey sandwich on homemade rye bread to Ruth.

Elizabeth handed her a cold glass of milk.

"Well, I see you think me helpless."

"Not at all, Ruth. We think you have been through a great trauma. As women, we know how much an emotional upset can drain one's energy," Elizabeth stated. "If you are going to find out what happened, you need your strength."

She smiled. "Thank you, Elizabeth. I was not very pleasant earlier, but Hattie talked some sense into me. I understand Cal is looking for him."

"He took a couple of friends from school with him. I wouldn't let him go alone." Hattie held out a chair and nudged Ruth toward it.

The sandwich revived her senses, and she savored every bite. "He went to the docks, didn't he?" The empty glass made a hollow sound on the wooden table as she set it down.

"It makes sense, Ruthie. All this madness is because of the mob. The only logical conclusion is Peter was taken hostage." Priscilla wheeled the chair closer to the table.

"Then, that is where I will go." She rose from the chair. "Oh, don't try to talk me out of it. He's there because of me. No one else should be in danger."

Everyone in the room protested.

Elizabeth pushed the boys out the back door. "Ruth, Charlie and Joseph are not aware of the danger. We need to be careful how we speak in front of them."

"Forgive me. I'm not accustomed to having young people around. Another lesson I need to learn, I guess. At any rate, the sandwich was wonderful, and I thank you. As soon as Cal returns with news, I will make my plans."

"Ruth, I don't think it is a good idea…"

"You have nothing to say about it, Mother." The room remained silent as she retired to the front porch to wait Cal's return.

Cal Taylor drove with both hands clutched tightly on the wheel. He had failed to spot anything at the docks—it was unusually quiet, but he listened to his buddies remind him of the night activity in that neighborhood. 'Yeah, yeah, I know. I'm frustrated about how much time is slipping away. Peter could be dead by now."

The friend in the back seat mumbled something under his breath.

"What did you say, Nick?"

"I said it's not Peter's death you need to worry about. Your mother was furious when we left. I've always been afraid of her, you know."

Cal laughed. "I can handle her, Nick. She tries to boss me around, but forgets I've been a grown man for many years now. I suppose it's because I still work at the college." A warm glow filled his heart. Hattie was exactly the spark he needed to convince him to leave there and start a life of his own. Ruth Squire took his fancy, at first, but when he saw Peter and Ruth together, he knew true love existed in this world. For a while, he mourned the loss, thought about fighting for her, but realized it would be futile. The night he met Hattie Morgenstern, at the boarding house, eradicated all thoughts of Ruth from his mind.

Still…a fondness for her remained, like a little sister. Peter proved himself a true friend, and he couldn't turn his back now.

"We'll grab a bite to eat, rest a few hours, and when the time is right, we'll head back to the docks. I'll park several blocks away. We walk into the lion's den," Cal stated.

"Are we going to need guns, Cal?" The second friend in the front passenger's seat spoke for the first time.

"I hope not, George, 'cause I don't own one."

No one spoke for the remainder of the ride to the boarding house.

An uneasy feeling settled over Cal the minute he pulled into the driveway. Ruth was sitting in a wicker chair on the front porch. She stood when the vehicle came to a stop. "Ruthie, I didn't expect you to be awake. How are you feeling? Better I hope."

Ruth was all business. "What did you find out, Cal? I want to know and don't hold anything back."

It was almost 5:30 p.m., and the guys were hungry. Cal didn't want to get into a long explanation about his plans for the night. "Whoa—let me introduce my friends from the school. This here is…"

"I already know George and Nick. I attended the school, too, in case you've forgotten. Stop stalling. I want to know everything." She crossed her arms and stared at Cal, ignoring the other two.

"Well, never you mind what I've forgotten or what I know, Miss Squire. Your little control act doesn't work on me. I'll tell you what I know after these boys have eaten." He turned to his friends. "Come on, the kitchen is this way."

He pretended not to notice the tears welling up in her eyes…those big brown eyes. The best thing he could do for her right now was to act tough. If he went soft, she would cave in, too.

"You look a mite puny, too, Ruthie. Have you eaten?" His voice reflected more concern than he wanted. "Look, I'll tell you what I know, which isn't much, while we eat. Come into the kitchen.

She brushed the tears away. "I've eaten."

His arm went protectively around her shoulders. "Have a cup of tea, then. We'll have a good talk."

Elizabeth rushed forward as the group entered the cozy kitchen, but Cal shook his head at her, and she retreated.

"Look, everyone. I'll inform you all together what I saw at the docks, but let my friends get something to eat. There is really not much to tell."

The cook bustled back and forth, and in the efficient way of practiced chefs, placed three sandwiches on the table. Elizabeth followed with cold glasses of milk.

Cal talked while the others wolfed down their food. "The docks were empty. We snooped around, but no one was about. Nothing to see. We're going to rest and head out late tonight when there should be more activity."

"I'm going with you," Ruth announced.

Everyone stopped and stared at Ruth.

Cal recovered first. "Oh no, you are not, young lady. The docks are no place for a woman, especially at night. The three of us can handle this."

She stamped her foot. "You can't stop me, Cal. If you won't take me with you, I'll go on my own." At the abrupt declaration, she turned and left the room.

No one said a word. Even Cal's friends stopped chewing to watch Ruth leave.

Elizabeth rushed toward him. "Cal, do something. We can't have Ruth running around the bad part of town at night. Short of locking her in the bedroom, I'm not sure we can stop her."

Priscilla Squire spoke from the far corner of the kitchen. "There will be no more of that, Elizabeth. She's too headstrong anyway. You can't keep her in a locked room. We need another idea."

"I'll talk to her. She listens to me," Hattie said.

Cal sat down with a sigh and grabbed his sandwich. "Good idea. I don't think I can handle an emotional woman and concentrate on finding Peter. You better go now, before she locks you out of the bedroom."

After Hattie disappeared up the stairs, Elizabeth turned to Cal. "Now, tell me what is really going on. I'm sure you know more than you are saying."

An Unlikely Beginning

Chapter Twenty-One

Peter stopped with a jerk. The raspy noise of weapons sliding out of holsters, the distinct click of the gun hammers, and the smiles he imagined on his captors faces made his blood run cold. He figured as much. They weren't going to let him walk out of here. His back stayed ramrod straight, and he stood perfectly still. "I thought you said I was your guest. Did you not understand what I said? I did not shoot your man."

Zapelli walked around to face Peter, putting them almost nose to nose. "I say you did."

The whiskey on Zapelli's breath almost made him gag, but he fought off the urge to flinch. "I guess we have a problem, then."

"I guess we do," Zapelli answered.

The air smelled of booze, cigars, and gun metal, and the room shrank as hostility grew. The silence continued, neither man willing to give in to the standoff.

"You want me to plug him, boss?" Moose finally broke the tension.

Zapelli laughed, the spell dissolved. "No, there ain't gonna be no killin' just yet." His gaze fixed on Adams. "The good captain here is gonna take him under his wing. I need runners. Kirby and Adams are dispensable, as far as I'm concerned. Because of them, I am a man short."

Adams came forward, the gun still in his hand, cocked and ready to fire. "Me? You said I could go if I delivered Kirby. Well, here he is."

"Put the gun away, Adams, before Moose puts a hole in ya. You'll go when I say you go. You ain't runnin' the show. You got a lot to learn about how this operation works." He jerked his head toward Moose. "Take 'em both upstairs and lock 'em in."

Moose waved the weapon at Adams, pushed Peter toward the door, and waited until the two men were both in the doorway.

Zapelli gave last minute instructions. "We move tonight. Get Fanny to bring them some grub, brief 'em on the operation, then it's lights out until midnight."

"Right, boss."

Peter noticed Adams was visibly shaken. Moose had grabbed Adam's gun and stuck it in his jacket. The captain turned white and stumbled as they climbed the stairs.

Moose put them both in an upstairs room, two bunks, one grimy window, and a bare light bulb dangling from the ceiling.

"This isn't the room I had before, Moose." Adams stood in the doorway and glanced around.

"That's right, Cappy. You and Kirby are gonna bunk together. Easier to keep an eye on the two of ya." Moose shoved him inside.

Peter followed Adams, silent, taking in the surroundings. *There isn't going to be much chance of escape.*

162

"Fanny will be up in a few shakes. Make yourselves comfy, I'll be back in an hour." Moose shut and locked the door.

"Looks like we're in this together, Adams." Peter walked around the room, hoping to spot anything to aid in an escape.

"Shut up, Kirby. If it wasn't for you, I'd be out of this mess," Adams shot back.

"You seem to have a short memory. I wasn't the one who pointed a gun at Mrs. Squire. I wasn't even there. It appears you have a knack for bad judgment." Peter sat down on the rickety bunk against the wall. "Guess this one is mine."

"How can you be so cavalier? They will probably never let us out of here. Sure, I made a mistake. I really loved Priscilla all those years ago." He paced like a nervous cat around the room. "I was young." He paused and looked out the filthy window. "She was so beautiful then. Hard to resist." He blinked and glared at Peter. "You would have done the same thing. Women can cast a spell on a man. I almost think they are devils."

"Whoa, there Adams. Don't lump me into that category. I've had plenty of opportunity with Ruth. I respect her too much to treat her like that. Who taught you that kind of behavior? Surely, not your mother." Peter balled his fists, ready to defend Ruth's honor.

The air seemed to have gone out of the captain's body. He slumped down on the other cot. "My mother was a saint. Prim, proper…she spoiled me. I loved her more than anything." A hard look crossed his face. "Father, on the other hand, was a scoundrel. He cheated on Mother constantly. When I was sixteen, he began to take me to places of ill repute. Said I needed to become a man." He stood, and the pacing started again. "I was confused. How could he treat Mother that way? I would try to ask him. He'd just say it's what a man does. Women know it and accept it. Stop being such a ninny."

Adams stood still in the middle of the room.

Quietly, Peter rose and stood next to the silent man. "I'm sorry Adams, I had no idea your father was that kind of a man." He put a hand lightly on the captain's forearm and whispered, "He was wrong, you know."

Adams hung his head and choked, tears spilling over the rims of his eyes. "I know. It was a confusing time for me." He jerked his arm away and wiped his eyes with the back of his hand. "When I realized Mother knew about Father's indiscretions and did nothing about it, my opinion of women changed. How could she allow it? Why didn't she stop him? Was it the money, the standing in the community? Was that all she was interested in? I couldn't process it."

A knock on the door and the sound of a key in the lock caused Adams to jerk away from Peter and move toward the window. Under his breath, he said, "You breathe a word of this to anybody, I'll kill you myself."

Fanny peeked around the half open door. "Alexander?"

Peter moved toward the door and reached out to take the tray from her hands. "He's here, miss, and so am I. I'm starving. What took you so long?"

"Now look here, mister. I don't know who you are, but nobody talks to Fanny Zapelli like that." She deftly evaded Peter's reach.

"Oh, I meant no harm, Fanny. Hunger makes a man a little testy." He bowed deeply." My apologies. Did you say your last name was Zapelli? Are you his wife?"

"Sister." She looked around Peter. "What are you doing, Alexander? I thought you would be glad to see me." The coffee cups rattled on the tray as she moved toward the captain.

Adams turned, smiling, all signs of emotion gone from his face. "Trying to see if there was any view out of this window, Fanny. You know I'm always glad to see you."

Fanny practically knocked Peter out of the way. "Well, that's better. I made this sandwich especially for you. I know how much you like roast beef."

Peter couldn't help but notice the softening lines in Adams face. *Something is going on here. I'll have to keep my eye on this. Could play into my escape.*

Fanny ignored Peter as she bustled around, setting up the tray on the bed, pushing Adams down, and positioning the white napkin over his lap. "Is the coffee too hot? I could get you something stronger to drink, if you like. Maybe you'd like your roast beef heated with gravy instead of cold. It would only take a minute…"

Adams took her hand. "It's fine, Fanny. Everything is fine. Please don't fuss so."

Peter saw the blush spread over her face and smiled. This is better than I figured. Fanny is smitten with him. I wonder if he feels the same.

Moose broke in. "Let's go, Fanny. The boss said not to talk to 'em. They gotta rest. The night shift will come early."

Adams withdrew his hand and grabbed the sandwich. "Go on, Fanny. I'm really tired. Think I'll eat and get some shuteye. We'll talk later."

Moose pulled Fanny toward the door. "I'll see you later, Alexander. Giovanni can't keep me away from you forever."

The door closed with a bang.

"Are you going to eat or stand there and stare at me?" Adams kept his eyes on his coffee cup.

"Yeah, I'm going to eat." Peter picked up a sandwich.

Neither man spoke.

The sandwiches disappeared one by one, and Peter studied Adam's face. If he was going to have any chance of getting out of this, he would have to win Adams over. The first step was to find out what was going on between him and Fanny Zapelli.

Finally, Adams cleared his throat, wiped the crumbs from his mouth with the napkin, and looked at Peter. "Thanks for giving me a minute when Fanny came in. I don't know what happened. Guess I'm not accustomed to talking about Mother and Father's misdeeds."

"It looks like we are in this together, Adams, whether we like it or not. I'm guessing Zapelli made you promises he had no intention of fulfilling. You may have noticed he did the same to me. We can either work together, or go it alone—up to you. My worry is that you will give me up because of Fanny. Want to tell me the story there?" Peter continued to sip the coffee.

"Nothing to tell. She comes waltzing into the club one day saying she was lonely — wanted to have some fun. Zapelli keeps a pretty tight rein on her. Doesn't let her have a boyfriend. She spotted me and begged him to let her take me out on the town. I never expected he'd go for it, but he did." Adams drained the last of his coffee. "We danced at some club called the Golden Nugget. You know, she's really a nice girl. Lonely. She wasn't used to high society manners, I suppose. I may be a bit of scoundrel myself, but I was taught how to treat a woman in public. She took a fancy to me."

Peter listened intently to the story. "You know, it could be to our advantage. It's possible she would be willing to help us when the time comes."

Adams shook his head. "Man, I don't want to get her involved. Deep down, she has a lot of good in her. That brother of hers holds her down. He hits her once in a while. She's probably afraid of him, even though he's her brother."

"Well, keep an open mind about it. I wouldn't deliberately put her in danger. If she wants out, this may be her ticket. The main thing is we need to work together, have each other's backs. I'm sure you don't want to end up in the river any more than I do." Peter put the cup down and stretched out on his bunk. "We need to get some shut eye. We'll have to be sharp tonight. You never know when we'll have an opportunity to run."

Adams studied Peter for a moment. "I'll think about it, but I don't want her hurt."

Peter closed his eyes. "Keep your mind on what you are going to do when you get out of here. You've got a

167

wife. Is it going to be Fanny or her? Make a decision, let me know which way you're going, and I promise I'll make it happen. It's just you and me, Adams."

Chapter Twenty-Two

Ruth tried to ignore the soft knock on the bedroom door, but the voice was Hattie's, pleading for a chance to talk. Resigned, she turned the bolt in the door.

"You won't change my mind, Hattie. I'm going down to the docks. He has to be down there. Where else could he have gone?"

"I'm not here to talk you out of it, Ruth. I only want you to wait until they have a chance to check it out. Did you even think you might be putting Cal and Peter in jeopardy by showing up down there?" Hattie went to the window, looked down at the garden, and whispered, "Ruth, I love him. I've really fallen in love with Cal. We're right for each other." She turned and reached for Ruth's hand. "Please, don't put him in danger, any more than he's going to be already. I can't stop him. He feels he owes Peter and won't rest until he finds him. We're both at risk of losing the men we love. Do it for me…do it for Peter and Cal."

Hattie's face bore the stress of the situation. Deep lines of worry creased her forehead. Ruth bowed her head. "I'm sorry, Hattie. It never occurred to me that you might be worried, too. There I go, only thinking of myself." A weak smile was all she could muster. "Of course, I'll wait." She stood and hugged her friend.

"Good, let's go down and tell the others. They are all worried about you."

Ruth pulled back. "Remember, if he sees anyone that remotely looks like Peter, I'm going down there myself."

Hattie laughed, softly. "As if I could stop you. We'll devise a plan, Ruthie. You and me, together. We'll find Peter and bring him back."

The kitchen hummed with conversation when the two women entered. Sidelong glances toward Ruth was all the notice anyone took. Even her mother continued conversation with Elizabeth.

"She's staying put, everyone. The agreement is to let Cal do a first go around. After that we'll make a collective decision as to how to proceed. For now, Ruthie stays here with us." Hattie pulled her into the room.

"Good idea," Cal said. "I'm glad you came to your senses, Ruth. You know I'll do everything I can to find him."

"I hope you find something, Cal, because if you don't, it will be my turn."

Priscilla Squire stood awkwardly. "Ruth, I think we should go back to the house tonight. There are some things I want to talk to you about."

"What things, Mother?"

"Private things. Things I should have shared with you long ago. It never seemed to matter before. Now, I think you should know."

"What about Cal? What if he finds Peter? I should be here when he gets back."

Elizabeth stepped in. "I'll be here, Ruth. I'm staying with Hattie until this whole thing is over. We've agreed. Cal will come and tell you everything. I think you should go home with your family."

Ruth looked from Elizabeth to her mother. "Well…"

"I'll drive you—on our way to the docks. It's really the best idea, Ruth," Cal said.

Priscilla Squire laid a soft hand on her shoulder. "Go get your father, dear. He's out on the back veranda. This has been such a strain on him. He's not been the same since the pneumonia. Sarah took the automobile home, a few hours ago, to ready the house for our return. It's best we go. Hattie has been more than gracious."

On the veranda, the night air was cold, but Father was wrapped in a warm overcoat petting Mrs. Whitewood's old Collie.

"Father, we're going home. Come inside before you get sick, again." Ruth bent down beside him.

"Home?"

"Yes, Cal is going to look for Peter, and we are going to give Hattie a bit of relief. There is nothing we can do here."

She noticed his feebleness as he stood and leaned a bit on her.

"I'd like to go home, Ruthie. I need some of that warm soup of Sarah's. That always makes me feel better. Where is your mother?"

"She's waiting for us inside. It was her suggestion."

The group made arrangements for Cal and his friends to rest in the parlor of the Squire's home until midnight, after which they would leave for the search on the docks.

It felt strange to be back in the house, her old room. She thought she would be a married woman by now, but instead, her life was chaos once again.

Sarah brought pillows and blankets, and the three men settled in the parlor to wait.

Priscilla called softly to her daughter through the closed door. "Ruth, come with me. It's time I showed you something."

She opened the door. "Where is Father? He seemed so frail tonight."

"Sarah has him all tucked into bed. He'll be right as rain tomorrow. It's time you and I had a woman to woman talk. I haven't been fair to you, and I want to make it right."

"Mother, none of this would have happened if I hadn't been so headstrong. I understand more now, truly I do." Ruth followed her into the hall.

"You understand nothing, Ruth, only what I have allowed you to know. There is so much more. Come with me." Mrs. Squire walked down the hall.

At her bedroom door she stopped and turned the knob. "I've kept this locked for so many years. Even your father didn't have access. Only Sarah knew the whole truth." She entered the bedroom.

Ruth followed, but protested, "Mother, I've seen the letters. I know about the incident with Captain Adams." She lowered her voice to a whisper. "I've even seen the dress. Sarah showed me."

Priscilla continued toward the closet, fished the key from the housedress, and opened the closet door. "That

172

is only the beginning, my child. I have much to tell you."

Without looking back, Priscilla disappeared into the closet. Ruth followed. The plain, sensible dresses made no sound as they moved past. When they turned the corner, she could smell the stale perfume and stopped.

Her mother turned and grabbed her hand. "Come, it's time you knew the truth."

Ruth was frightened. The truth? What truth?

The beautiful dresses were all there, the shoes and gloves to match. Ruth figured Sarah would have hidden them away, but she supposed Sarah would not have thought Ruth would be back here.

The letters still lay upon the vanity, scattered, where she had left them.

"I've read them, Mother, as you can see. I know everything."

"No, you don't know the rest of the story." Priscilla Squire pulled open the top door, undid a latch on the inside, and opened a hidden compartment. "You didn't find these."

Ruth stared at the handful of notes in her mother's hand. A red ribbon was wrapped around them, much like the others she'd found. These had not been opened, however.

"What are those, Mother? Who are they from, Captain Adams? I know how he tried to deny his role in the assault. I read it in those letters." She pointed to the scattered parchments on the dresser. "Did you love him? How could you love him after what he did? Has your life with Father been a lie?" Ruth's anger bubbled to the top.

Priscilla sat down, pulled on the ribbon, and watched it fall to the floor.

Suddenly, Ruth didn't want to know, turned her back, and stamped her foot. "I won't hear it, I tell you. How could you do it to Father?"

Softly, Priscilla began the story. "These letters are not from Captain Adams, Ruthie. They are from Baldassare Zapelli."

Chapter Twenty-Three

"Get up!"

Peter woke to the sound of Moose yelling at Adams and kicking Peter's bed. The light in the window had dimmed to dark. *I must have fallen asleep, after all.*

Adams grumbled at Moose. "Okay, okay, I'm up."

"What time is it, anyway?" Peter reached for his pocket watch, but remembered it was in his wedding jacket.

"Time to learn your job, punk. Get these on and follow me downstairs." He threw some dark clothes at the men and waited in the hall.

Adams and Peter hurried to pull on the coats and hats. Peter attempted to shake the sleep from his brain. Clear wits were essential for any escape effort. He knew, by this time, Ruth would be a mess, his mother would be distraught, and he hoped Cal was looking for him. Every move he made, he needed to be alert and ready for action. Whether Adams was ready remained to be seen.

Downstairs, 'The Nose' sat in a club chair, leaned back, smiling—watching as they descended the stairs. "Hope you had a good rest, boys. We got work to do."

Adams started to complain. "Look boss, I'm not one to do manual labor. I've always been one to give orders. Just what is it we are doing?"

Moose snorted a laugh.

"Shut up, Moose. We have a situation on our hands. The good Captain isn't used to grunt work. Wonder what we should do about that?"

"I have an idea, boss. We give him a gun to hold on Kirby, whilst he loads the boats. He can shoot him if he tries anything funny," Moose offered.

Zapelli looked long and hard at his hired gun. "You know, that's not a bad idea, Moose. That way, they couldn't pin Kirby's murder on us. Sometimes, you surprise me."

Moose grinned like a Cheshire cat, obviously happy he had pleased the boss.

"Yeah, that's exactly what we will do. Kirby is used to hard work, got the muscles to prove it. Adams here can be his jailer. Okay, let's do this."

Moose waved the gun at Adams and Peter. They moved through the kitchen and out the back door, into an alley. The path led down to the river.

Very little light illuminated the dock, but even from his vantage point, Peter could see the water was murky and it looked very cold. A small, beat up rowboat was bobbing up and down, tied to the dock.

Peter hesitated. "That's what we're going in? Do you see how choppy the water is? The boat could capsize."

"Not my problem. I won't be in the boat," Moose replied. "Adams is gonna hold the gun on ya. Either you drown or he shoots ya. Makes no difference to me. And if you do make it to the other side, Mac's over there waitin' on ya. Just a little insurance that you don't run."

Adams and Peter looked at each other. Peter knew the wheels were turning in Adams head. This didn't look good for either one of them. They couldn't swim for it, the water was too cold. Adams couldn't shoot him. Who would row the boat? He was sure, the captain had never steered a ship in his life, much less a rowboat. If the boat capsized, they would both be goners, for sure. It was best for them to work together until they got to the other side. Would Adams get that message?

"So, what's the plan, Moose?" Adams asked.

"You boat over to the other side, pick up the goods, and bring 'em back here. Simple."

Three men surrounded Adams and Peter. Moose handed Adams a gun. "Here's your piece. Don't get too jumpy with it. Plug him if he gets stupid."

Both men climbed into the boat, Adams hand shaking with the weight of the pistol.

"Wait!"

It was Zapelli. He tossed a small, cloth bag into the boat. "Make sure these get to the contact."

Peter caught the bag and tucked it under the wooden seat. From the feel of it, he knew it was stolen jewelry. He scanned the shore for a sign of help, but was disappointed. No police, no Cal. There had to be a chance, something, somewhere that he could use to escape. The last thing in the world he thought he would ever be doing was smuggling.

When the boat was out of earshot from the shore, Adams looked at Peter. "What do we do now?"

Peter rowed while the captain held the gun loosely in his hand. He hoped it wouldn't accidentally go off.

177

"We do what they say for now. I don't see we have much choice. I'm not sure what's on the other side. They said the one they called Mac was over there waiting for us. I'm assuming we pick up the liquor and bring it back. Maybe after a couple of runs they will let us go."

"They aren't letting us go." Adams said in a quiet voice.

"Yeah, well, we'll have to make our own plans. We have to keep our wits about us. Don't panic. Look for an opportunity. Think you can do that, Adams?"

In the moonlight, Adams face looked stark and pale. Fear shone in his eyes, but he nodded. "I think so."

"Look, this is a chance to redeem yourself from the past. If we pull this off, get out alive, I'll vouch you were the hero, clear your name and reputation. But, I have to count on you. You have to be one hundred percent committed to the plan."

Adams looked over Peter's shoulder to the shore approaching. It was clear he was scared, frightened to death.

"Watch me, Adams. Try not to react until I give you a sign. We might have to make this trip several times before I find the trick to our escape. Can you hang in there with me?"

Adams nodded, and Peter kept rowing.

Cal nudged his friends awake. It was midnight, time to head to the docks. He hadn't slept any, tried to make a plan. The fact the gang would be armed, and he and his friends had no guns worried him. They would have to keep out of sight, not stir up any suspicions. All their lives depended on it. He had no idea where to get pistols, and it was probably the best idea not to have any. Someone might get trigger happy. No…stealth would have to be their weapon, that, and a plan to outsmart them.

The house was quiet, and he assumed everyone was upstairs, asleep. They closed the door quietly and made sure it was locked. Traffic on the streets was non-existent this time of night. They didn't speak much, Cal knew each one had their own thoughts, each one understood the danger.

Cal found a spot to park. No one moved, at first, then, with a sigh, Cal opened his door, put on his jacket, and motioned for the others to follow.

The rubber soles of their shoes made no sound as they trudged along the back street. The night was dark, no moon, only the occasional street lamp to light their way. Grateful for the dark, Cal relaxed a little, confident they were virtually invisible.

The river dock came into view, and Cal could see movement along the shoreline. They chose an alley, and inched their way as close as they could.

"Shouldn't we spread out, Cal?" George whispered, his collar was pulled up over his ears, and the wool cap hid his eyes.

"I don't think so. It's better if we stay together. I don't plan on facing these goons tonight. We're sort of casing the joint, see if we can spot Peter anywhere. Keep your eyes peeled, I told you what he looks like, he should be easy to pick out from the rest of them."

Cal moved forward, hiding behind boxes stacked in the alley, his muscles tensed with anticipation.

Nick joined the chorus, "You ain't getting me to split up. I'm sticking with Cal. Strength in numbers, I always say."

"Shh," Cal put a finger to his lips. "No more talking, just watch what's going on."

As his eyes adjusted to the dark, he could see more and more men bustling back and forth near the water. The problem was, they all wore dark clothing, too. It was hard to tell what any of them looked like. They seemed to be unloading something from the boats tied to the dock.

All of a sudden, one stood out. Cal clapped George on the arm. "Look," he whispered. "The one on the end—holding a gun. Look at the way he stands, erect, square shouldered. I can't see the color of his hair, but I'd swear he doesn't look like he belongs in that group. Do you see him?"

George grunted an affirmation. "Look at the guy next to him. He keeps looking around…like he is going to bolt. The square-shouldered one glances around, too. Seems to me, if the one was guarding the other, he'd notice the other guy's nervousness. What do you make of it, Cal?"

"Do you see those barrels over there? Let's see if we can get a little closer. Stay low, and follow me."

Slowly, like alley cats, they shuffled the few yards to the barrels. With the better vantage point, Cal studied the two men in question. He waited, hoping the nervous man would look in his direction. After a few minutes, the man looked square at him. Only Cal was hidden behind the barrel. He saw his full face. It was Peter.

"It's him, it's Peter. We found him." Cal kept his voice low, not wanting the night air to carry the sound down wind.

"Now what, Cal? They have guns. We can't rush 'em." Nick's voice shook with fear.

"Don't worry, Nick, we aren't going to rush them. I need to hear what they are saying. We have to get closer."

Cal looked around, praying he could find something to hide behind, close enough to hear the voices. At the end of the dock, a truck was parked as if waiting for cargo. Two men with guns acted as guards. It was his only option.

"You two stay here; I'm going to make for that truck. Only one of us can pull it off. There's not enough room for all of us. You'll be able to see me, so stay down."

"No Cal, it's too risky. What if they see you? They'll kill you on the spot," George protested.

"I've got to get close enough to hear what they are saying. I can't leave Peter here without knowing the plan. We have no choice."

Before any further protests could be voiced, Cal crouched and sprinted to the back of the truck. He'd guessed right. Now, he could hear them talking.

"Do ya think the boss is going to plug 'em tonight, Mac?" The big one with no neck asked his partner.

"Nah, we got ten more loads to get. We won't get that done tonight. I figure he'll use 'em until we get the job done, then he'll plug 'em." He laughed. "Oh, and don't forget about the girls. We got about five broads who want to peddle to those Canadians. The boss will want those guys to escort 'em, if you know what I mean."

Both men laughed, but kept their eyes on the activity near the dock.

It was all Cal needed to hear. They were using Peter, and some other guy, to make the illegal runs. Obviously, they were dispensable to the operation. He wondered how many more loads they would be expected to make. Well, he'd have to figure only one more night. Peter would be safe until then. He ached to get a message to his friend, let him know he was on the case, trying to figure a rescue. The chance was too great. All he could do was pray.

He waited to see if they spoke about any details of the operation, but they turned their conversation to women. Cal looked behind him. His friends were tucked out of sight behind the barrels. The two thugs concentrated on the water. It was now or never.

He crab-crawled to the edge of the alley and motioned Nick and George to follow him.

Once more out of earshot, he explained the situation to his friends.

"You mean we have to come back? Can't we figure a way to get him out tonight? Geesh, Cal, this is creepy. We could get shot," Nick complained.

They walked back to the automobile. "Neither one of you is obligated in any way to help me. I can't risk not having a solid plan before I go rushing in there to save Peter. So you are off the hook. I appreciate you having my back tonight, and I don't expect you to put yourselves in any more danger."

Nick and George climbed into the vehicle and stayed silent while Cal drove toward Ruth's house. He figured the best thing to do was stay the rest of the night there and face whatever plan he came up with in the morning.

In the back seat, Nick cleared his throat as if to speak.

"You got something to say, Nick?" Cal looked at him through the rearview mirror.

"Aw, Cal, it's that I met this girl. We're going to be married. I don't want anything to mess it up. I gotta think of her, too, you know."

Cal nodded his head, but kept his eyes on the road. "You don't have to explain, Nick. You proved yourself more than my friend tonight. I will forever be in your debt. You have my blessing. I'll take you back to the bus station in the morning." He looked over at George. "Unless George is going back, too. In which case, he can drive the both of you home."

"You better get that bus ticket, Nick. I'm staying with Cal."

Cal was more than a little relieved to hear George announce his intentions. He sure could use the back up. "Thanks, George," he whispered.

The house came into view, and Cal could see a light in the window. There was no doubt who waited for him in the parlor.

An Unlikely Beginning

.

Chapter Twenty-Four

Ruth and Sarah sat in the parlor, teacups on their laps, in total silence. Sleep would not come. She didn't think sleep would ever come again. Peter's disappearance and Mother's revelation had drained her of emotion, numbed her, and rendered her incapable of rational thought. Sarah found her sitting on the stairs sobbing into her nightdress.

"Ah, she told you then, did she?" Sarah draped a robe around Ruth's shaking shoulders. Did she tell you the whole of it, then?"

All Ruth could do was nod and gulp, trying to hold back the flood of tears. "She killed someone, Sarah. My mother is a…"

"Well, and it was bound to come out sooner or later, dearie. I'm of a mind she should have told ya sooner. Alas, it's her way to keep secrets, and it's not for me to have a say." She pulled Ruth to her feet. "Come on now, I suspect you need a spot of my hot cocoa to rouse ya."

She fell in step, slowly, beside the little maid, like the old days when Sarah would comfort her after a scraped knee or bee sting. Whatever will power was left in her disappeared at Mother's confession. Peter was gone, maybe dead, and she had received the shocking news her mother was a murderess.

185

The kitchen, the safe haven in the house, always soothed a battered spirit. Sarah not only kept it spotless, but added warmth and hospitality to the room. Large plants in the windows, colorful curtains, spices simmering on the stove to fill the room with a welcoming atmosphere. She'd brought the secrets of her homeland to the Squire's kitchen. It didn't hurt that she was a superb cook. Ruthie had never known anything but the finest cuisine. One thing stood out more than the rest, however. Cocoa. Sarah made the best homemade cocoa, ever. The secret was closely guarded and no amount of persuasion would convince Sarah to reveal it.

Ruth closed her eyes and let the warm, chocolate aroma fill her wounded spirit. The slow, rhythmic scrape of the metal spoon in the saucepan filled the room and drove away the negative air.

"She didn't kill him, ya know." Sarah spoke softly, eyes concentrating on the bubbling brew.

Ruth wasn't sure she heard her correctly. "What did you say?"

Eyes riveted on the sauce pan, she repeated, "She didn't kill him, Ruthie."

"You're wrong—she told me, the whole story."

"She was covering for me. I killed him."

"Why would she cover for you? It wasn't your problem, Sarah."

"I would have been deported, or worse. She wouldn't let that happen."

Finally, Sarah looked up from the pot, pulled it off the stove, and poured two mugs full. "When your ma found out she was with child, she nearly had a breakdown. It would ruin her family, a huge disgrace. She tried to find Cap'n Adams, but his father put him out to sea. Pulled all kinds of strings, made him a captain in the navy, he did. So, Priscilla went to his father."

Ruth nodded as she sipped the steaming chocolate. "Yes, she told me that much."

"Mr. Adams was furious. Not with his son, but with your ma. Threatened her, said he would ruin her and the family if she spread the rumor. Priscilla argued with him, stood her ground, but he would hear none of it. She couldn't tell her parents. They knew nothing about the attack." Sarah stared into her cup and stirred. "She didn't know I followed her."

"You followed her, why?"

"She was all alone, Ruthie. No one knew anything about any of it, but me. I had to make sure I could protect her."

"What happened after that? How did Baldassare Zapelli get mixed up with my mother?"

"Did she show you those letters, too?" Sarah stopped stirring. "Mr. Adams. He hired Zapelli to kill her."

Ruth shivered. "They wanted to kill Mother…and me?"

"Och, child—it wasn't you she carried in her belly. No, there was a miscarriage. She lost that child."

Ruth was stunned. "She said…I thought…"

"You didn't hear her out, Ruthie. She didn't finish the story. All you heard was that she killed someone."

"Suppose you finish it, then."

187

"It's simple. Adams put a hit on her. He hired the mob. Baldassare Zapelli, to be exact. I know a little of gangsters, ya know—from where I come from. With the power Adams wielded in this town, I guessed what might come next. Priscilla was going to put the truth out there and ruin the Adams name. He couldn't let her do that. He had too much to lose."

Ruth pushed the cocoa aside. "So how did it happen, Sarah…that you killed Zapelli?"

Sarah got up from the table and rinsed the cup in the sink. "I made sure she didn't go anywhere alone. Oh to be sure, she was none the wiser, and never knew I followed her. It was hard sometimes, because of her parents. They were innocent in all of the unpleasantness. Your ma kept it well hidden, but she knew, sooner or later, her growing belly would need an explanation. She hoped to get Mr. Adams to fetch Alexander back to marry her before it was too late. Instead, the days went by, and she began to panic."

"She went to Adams house again?"

"No, her thought was to get the police involved. Silly of her I know, but she wasn't thinking right. On her way, Baldassare Zapelli pulled her into an alley, held a knife to her throat. If I hadn't been there, he would have slit it, sure as I'm standin' here."

"Zapelli? Why does that name sound familiar? I've heard it somewhere." Ruth stood. "How did you stop him, and for goodness sake, where was Father in all of this? I thought he was to marry her after the attack."

"Yes, he wanted to marry her. Your ma knew the baby wouldn't look like your pa. Both your parents are dark haired. Alexander is blond, tall, altogether different looking. She just plain didn't want the truth to come out."

Ruth sat down and rubbed her forehead. "Please tell me everything, Sarah. I'm so confused."

Sarah came across the room and patted her head like in the old nursery days. "That day, in the alley…I threw this at Baldassare." Her hand fumbled in her apron pocket and drew out a short, curved knife."

Ruth gasped. "A knife? Oh Sarah…"

"I told you in the hospital, my father sent me here well-prepared." She slipped the knife back into the pocket.

"First the gun, now a knife—what other weapons do you carry?"

Sarah tried to hide the grin. "That's it—the little gun and the throwing knife."

"What if you had missed? You would both be dead. Tell me how he died, Sarah."

The morning grew lighter, even though the sun was not yet up. Both women jumped at the sound of a key in the door.

In an instant, Ruth's attention flashed to the current situation. Peter. "It's Cal. Maybe he's found him." She ran to the front door, Sarah close behind.

The door swung open slowly, and Cal's head peeked around the door frame. When he saw Ruth, he looked relieved. "Good, you're up."

"Did you find him, Cal? Where is he?"

Cal and the other two brushed by her and went straight to the kitchen. "I need coffee."

"But, Cal…"

"I think we saw him, Ruthie. Too dark to be sure." He turned to seek out Sarah, but she was at the stove, already pouring three cups of coffee.

Ruth grabbed his arm. "Why didn't you get him? How could you leave him there like that?"

This time, Sarah spoke up, loud and in control. "Ruthie, it's time you shut up and let the man speak. We're talkin' about the mob here. You don't waltz in and take what they think is theirs. Isn't that right, Cal?" She held the mug out for him to take.

Ruth sat down, stunned.

"Ah, Ruth," Cal said, his voice soft and kind. "Don't you know I would have brought him if I could? They all had guns. We were no match for them. It's time to make a plan. By the conversation, I think he will be safe until tomorrow night."

"Tomorrow?"

They all turned at a rap on the main door.

Sarah responded first. "Who could be knockin' at this hour?"

Ruth went to the door and found Hattie and Elizabeth standing there holding hands, fear shining in their eyes.

"Did you find him?" Elizabeth spoke first.

Ruth shook her head. "Cal believes he saw him at the docks, but the place was swarming with men armed with guns."

Elizabeth gasped, and Hattie wrapped an arm around her shoulder.

Sarah appeared, ushered the women in, and took their coats. "Come to the kitchen, it seems the only place anyone wants to be at this terrible time."

"Where are the boys, Elizabeth?" Ruth asked.

"Cal's mother said she would keep an eye on them. Of course, they are asleep. I expect I should go back and get them before they wake."

From the back of the room, Cal waved his hand. "I'll take care of it, Elizabeth. I need to get fresh clothes, anyway. Nick is heading back to the school. George will stay with me until we devise a plan."

Sarah already cracked eggs and was making toast at Cal's announcement. "Ya won't be leavin' my kitchen on an empty stomach, Cal. You hold on til you eat a proper breakfast. Ruth—you take Elizabeth up to the guest room. Hattie I'd like you stay with Ruthie for a bit, until I get the meals straightened out. I might not be able to help find Peter, but I can keep the rest of you strong."

Cal smiled gratefully at Sarah. "You are a life saver. I am starving."

Nick and George wasted no time attacking their plates, either.

"Come ladies, I need to look in on Mother. I'll get everyone settled upstairs. Elizabeth, you look exhausted." Ruth took both women's hands and led them down the hall to the stairs.

After Ruth was satisfied her mother and father were sleeping, she turned back the coverlet for Elizabeth in the guest room, and left her to rest.

She practically dragged Hattie down the hall to her bedroom, closed the door, and locked it.

"What are you locking the door for, Ruth? Afraid I might run out on you?"

"No time for jokes, Hattie. There is nothing Cal can do without putting himself in real danger. It's up to us. You and me."

"What in blazes are you talking about? There isn't anything we can do. We're women, and we have no guns."

Ruth put her hands on her hips and smiled. "We don't need guns."

Hattie shook her head. "You've lost your mind, Ruth. Are we going to point our finger at them, and they all fall down dead?"

"Of course not, we sing."

"Sing," Hattie stated flatly.

"The Blue Feather Saloon is down on the docks. That's got to be the place they are holding Peter. Remember? All the blue feathers, the threats? It's the only logical place."

A light brightened in Hattie's eyes. "Are you saying we go down there and get hired as singers?"

"That's exactly what I'm saying. If we dress the part, no one will recognize us. You can't tell me you don't sing, Hattie Morgenstern. I've heard you around the piano. You have a great voice."

Hattie giggled. "Those were classical songs. I took lessons in my home country, but I've never tried any jazz songs. I'm not sure I could pull it off."

Ruth sat on the bed and crossed her legs. "If we dress the part, no one will care what we sound like."

Shock registered on Hattie's face. "Dress the part — you mean dress like...?"

"You're getting the idea."

"What about you? Have you ever belted out a song in a place like that?"

The thought struck a chord of fear, but Ruth recovered. "I've always wanted to be an actress…now is my chance." A weak smile was all she could muster.

The room grew silent, but Ruth knew Hattie well enough by now. She would take the challenge. After all, Peter was once her betrothed.

Finally, Hattie broke the spell. "What about Cal? He'll never let me do it."

"He won't know. While he's busy devising his plan, we'll be off putting ours into action."

"I can't lie to him, Ruth. We can't start our relationship on a lie." Hattie shook her head.

Ruth lowered her voice and stared straight into Hattie's eyes. "Do you want Peter to die?"

That did the trick.

"No. Of course not."

"After Cal leaves to get changed and pick up the boys, we sneak into Mother's closet, and find something we can use to dress like women who…well, who sing in nightclubs. With all of Mother's old clothes, we can surely find something."

Hattie hesitated.

Ruth stood and went to the door. "If you won't do it with me, Hattie, I'll do it by myself."

An Unlikely Beginning

Chapter Twenty-Five

Peter was beat. The boat ride across the water wasn't the hard part. The loading and unloading the crates of liquor was. Even though he was physically fit from his milk route business, his muscles ached. Adams wasn't as bad off as he was, though. All he had to do was hold the gun.

After the first load, they sent them back again, this time with a couple of 'ladies'. Peter felt dirty, sad, and disgusted all at the same time. He was no prude, but it was obvious what these ladies were going over there to do. It went against his grain to be a part of it. The only thing that kept him sane was knowing he had to stay alive to get back to Ruth, his mother and the boys. He couldn't be sure what these guys would do to his family if he wasn't around. They had done two loads tonight and dawn was breaking. He'd heard someone say ten loads was the order. That gave him a couple more nights to figure out a plan.

"You did good, Kirby," Mac stated. "Most of 'em fall out before the last load—faint dead away. You kept up real good. The boss will approve."

"Glad to hear it," Peter said.

"Moose said to bring you to the kitchen when you finish. Fanny will fix you up something to eat. You'll sleep most of the day tomorrow and start all over again." Mac laughed like he'd told a hilarious joke.

"Fine," Peter mumbled. The mention of Fanny's name changed Adam's appearance. He'd figured it right, Fanny might be their ticket out.

"Gimme the gun, Captain." Mac held out his hand.

"But…" Adams mumbled.

"You'll get it back tomorrow, now move."

The walk back to The Blue Feather was the longest Peter could remember. He was weak with hunger, and all the muscles in his body screamed for rest.

Inside, Fanny, adorned with apron and spatula, was busy at the stove. Her eyes lit up when Adams entered. Once more, Peter smiled to himself.

Fanny pointed the spatula at Mac. "You're working him too hard. Look at him. He's about to pass out. How can he go dancing with me, if he's worked to the bone?"

"Aw, Fanny, he didn't do nothin' but hold the gun on Kirby. Lay off. Why you want a cream puff like him is beyond me, when I'm the best thing goin'." Mac winked.

"Oh, not you, too, Mac. Moose hands me that line almost every day. Why would I want the likes of either one of you?" She turned back to the grill. "Sit down, Captain, I'll have your food in a sec."

Peter was about to ask if he was included in her culinary talents when Mac spoke first.

"Hey, what about me and Kirby, here? We need to eat, too."

"Shut up and sit down, Mac. I'll have yours in a jiffy. The Captain is first." She slid a full plate of steak, eggs, and onions across the counter to Adams.

Peter's mouth watered. A growl rose from the depths of his belly at the sight of the food. *For thugs, they sure eat well.*

The next plate was for Mac, and it was obvious he was low man on the pole.

Fanny kept a stream of conversation going with Adams, and he wondered what the good captain saw in her. She was uncouth, talked like one of the guys, and the constant gum snapping would definitely get on his nerves.

Finally, the meal was consumed, and Peter felt the need for sleep. He hoped he could make it up the stairs before he collapsed from pure exhaustion.

Adams lingered in the kitchen with Fanny, and Mac didn't seem to object. Peter hoped he would get to talk strategy, but knew he would be sound asleep before Adams made it up the stairs. He couldn't even think about anything but the rickety bed, and his head hitting the pillow.

The next morning came and went without Peter's knowledge. He'd fallen into the deepest sleep he'd known in a long time. By noon, he was being kicked awake by Moose.

"You've had enough sleep, Kirby. You need to get down to the kitchen and get some grub so we can get the plan for the night laid out."

Peter looked around. "Where's Adams?"

"Already down there, talking to Fanny."

He didn't like the look on Moose's face. The jealousy between the two could put a monkey wrench in his plans for escape.

Moose broke his cardinal rule and expressed personal feelings. "If I could get away with it, I'd plug him right now, but the boss would probably plug me." He kicked a chair. "Hurry up, Kirby; my mood isn't gettin' any better."

So far, he hadn't had a chance to talk to Adams and form a plan. If there was to be any chance, it had to be today. Maybe in the boat…

Downstairs, Adams was leaned over the counter laughing and flirting with Fanny, which didn't help Moose's mood. His mottled face turned a dark red.

"Get Kirby's grub, Fanny, we're in a hurry."

She frowned. "Don't rush me, Moose. I'll get it when I am good and ready."

"Yeah, maybe the boss would like to hear you say that." Moose's look changed to a smug smile.

Peter let them hash things out and tried to absorb the innuendo's flying back and forth. He began to wonder if Fanny really had a thing for Moose and was trying to make him jealous. It was hard to tell the way her eyes lit up when Adams entered the room. At any rate, he'd keep an eye on this situation.

The food was served. Moose tapped his foot impatiently while Peter ate.

"Where's my gun, Moose?" Adams forced his eyes from Fanny.

"You better watch your step, or I'll change it up, and let Kirby hold it today," Moose answered.

A stricken look passed over the captain's face, and Peter almost laughed out loud.

The suggestion was enough to get Adams to move away from the counter and find a table in the corner of the room. He put his feet on the tabletop and watched from afar.

Peter kept his head down and concentrated on his food, but took in the play by play between the others. He also noticed 'The Nose' hadn't made an appearance. This could be good, or it could be bad.

Moose's patience ran out. He barked at Peter, "You've had enough. Let's go."

He pushed the plate away. "Thanks Fanny, that was excellent, as always."

She took a second look at him, as if seeing him for the first time. A nod was all she gave him, but he saw a hint of a smile.

While they headed to the back room, Peter decided to try to get Fanny on his side. She seemed to respond to good manners — one more thing to use as a weapon.

The more time passed, the more he dreaded the long night ahead. One slip up and he could end up at the bottom of the river.

"What are we picking up, tonight, Moose?" he ventured.

"Dunno, boss hasn't given the order, yet."

Peter tried to stretch the opportunity to get more information. "Where is he? Thought he'd be all over this, today."

"He's up in his office doing business. That's all you gotta know. Get in there and sit down. We'll know soon enough."

He looked around, tried to spot anything resembling a weapon. A cabinet in the corner looked

199

promising. There wasn't a lock on it, and something told him it might contain what he was looking for. He hoped he would be left alone long enough to investigate.

Adams remained quiet, and Moose stood guard. Peter kept watch on his surroundings.

A few minutes later, Zapelli came strolling through the door. Behind him, three questionable looking women, wearing feathers and sequins, followed close on his heels, giggling between themselves. Peter's heart sank.

Chapter Twenty-Six

Ruth and Hattie looked at each other. Cal and his friends left for the boarding house, evident by the bang of the front door.

"We have to go now, Hattie. Mother is asleep, thanks to the medicine the doctor prescribed. She won't hear us. Once we're in the closet, we're safe."

"Can't we go through the guest room?"

"No, Elizabeth is in there, and she hasn't taken any medication. We have to go through the closet in Mother's room."

Hattie sighed, but followed Ruth into the hall.

Ruth stopped. "Are you sure you are one hundred percent on board with this?"

"Even if I weren't, I couldn't let you go alone, Ruth. I just wish we could tell Cal."

"No sense in worrying anyone else. Come on."

They tiptoed into Priscilla Squire's room, stopped to see if she stirred, and continued to the closet. Ruth took out the key and unlocked the door. Careful to close it without a sound, she motioned for Hattie to follow her. Around the corner and there they were...those beautiful dresses.

"You've never been here, have you, Hattie?"

"No, only heard about it. It's unbelievable. So many colors, it's beautiful, but they are from another era. How are we going to make them look like they belong to today's fashion?"

Ruth hadn't thought that far ahead. "I don't suppose we can ask Sarah to help. She'd try to stop us."

"I've done a little sewing, maybe between us we can fashion something." She started to thumb through the dresses.

Ruth started on the other end. Most of the dresses had long full skirts with low cut bodices, very dated and out of style. It was discouraging, to say the least, but it was the only place she knew to find something suitable.

She let out a yelp as she made her way to the back left corner.

Hattie jumped. "Did you find something?"

"Yes, look at this. With a little adjustment, this would work perfectly."

She held out the hangar and pulled off the dust cover.

Hattie sucked in her breath.

The dress was a vibrant royal blue velvet, strapless, with a long, straight skirt. Ruth rummaged around the floor and emerged triumphant. Matching blue velvet open-toed heels.

Hattie went to the top shelf and found the long, blue satin gloves.

"I thought I looked through all these dresses, I've never seen this one before." Ruth ran her hand over the soft material. "This one is it, Hattie. I can make this work."

"I agree, but I hope it's not too perfect. These people are ruthless and will kill at the drop of a hat. They are gangsters, after all."

Her voice lowered to barely a whisper. "I know, Hattie, I know."

The solemn mood was broken by Hattie's declaration. "Now, we have to find something for me."

Ruth hung the blue velvet on the vanity mirror and dove in to find something for her friend. It had to be right, it had to be convincing.

Eventually, they found a red satin gown, strapless, like the blue velvet—slinky, with a long skirt. Hattie was sure she could nip the waist and shorten it to make it work.

When and where had Mother worn these gowns? They don't fit with the rest of them. Even more curious, why?

Quietly, they left the closet, crept past the sleeping Mrs. Squire, and hurried back to Ruth's bedroom. For the next two hours, the girls ripped, stitched, and adjusted the gowns until they reached the desired effect. Time was of the essence. The Squire's rose about nine o'clock, Sarah would call for breakfast, and Cal will be bringing the boys home any minute.

Ruth stood in front of the mirror.

"Gosh, Ruth, you look older, maybe twenty. You are so beautiful in that color."

"Is it too much? Maybe I should tone it down some. I want to draw attention, but not the wrong kind, if you know what I mean."

"Take off the head band and the feather. Leave your hair unadorned. I think it would make you look more vulnerable, not so worldly." Hattie adjusted her own gown.

She removed the headband, straightened her hair, and turned to Hattie for approval.

"That's it. Perfect."

It was Hattie's turned for inspection.

"Let's leave the headband, but take off the feather. Red is so much more suggestive, don't you think?" Ruth pulled the feather from the band.

In silence, they stared at the reflection until they heard an automobile pull in front of the house and the squeal of Peter's brothers as they ran up the stairs.

Elizabeth's voice drifted up as she greeted her sons. "I've missed you!"

"Oh, Mother, it's only been overnight," Charles complained.

The girls scrambled to undress, hide their contraband in the closet, and hurry to dress in regular clothes.

"Are you sure we can pull this off?" Hattie whispered at the bottom of the stairs.

"We have no choice," Ruth answered.

Everyone was in the kitchen except the Squire's.

"Where are Mother and Father?" Ruth asked Sarah.

"Your pa took her breakfast in bed. She had a restless night, something about bad dreams," Sarah said.

The girls exchanged glances.

Ruth changed the subject. "Cal, did you come up with a plan?"

"I called the police, no help there, said they'd arrest him if he was smuggling." Cal brought a hot cup of coffee to his lips and sipped gingerly.

"Arrest him!? He was kidnapped, forced to go with those thugs. Why can't they get that through their heads?" Ruth stood in the doorway, fists clenched.

No one answered.

Cal finished his coffee and walked toward the sink. "George and I are going back down there tonight." He hesitated. "I've got a gun."

Hattie gasped. "Cal, no…"

Elizabeth took up the plea, "Please, Cal, don't put yourself in danger, don't take a gun."

He smiled, put the cup down with a clatter, and hurried to put an arm around Hattie. "I'll be fine. Now, I need some sleep. Okay if we stay in the parlor?" he asked Ruth.

Elizabeth interjected, "Take the guest room, Cal. I didn't sleep, the bed isn't even mussed. I only sat in the chair and stared out the window."

Ruth looked at Hattie. Had Elizabeth heard them in the closet? No… she would have said something.

"Is that okay, Ruthie?" Cal asked.

"Yes, of course. George, you can sleep on the sofa in the parlor if you are too crowded up there," Ruth answered.

George looked relieved. "Yes, ma'am. I'll take the sofa."

Cal kissed Hattie on the cheek and headed upstairs, George trudged toward the parlor, and Sarah busied around the kitchen making breakfast for the rest of them.

Everyone was around the large butcher block table when Elizabeth spoke, "What about Cal's mother? We can't just leave her there. She has to be worried about him. We've gone off and left her alone."

Sarah looked up from the frying pan. "Ruth, why don't you and Hattie go pick her up and bring her here."

"No!" Ruth almost shouted. "I mean, no, I can't leave here. Peter might come here first if he manages to get away. You always like driving the auto Sarah, why don't you go this time. Hattie and I will clean up here."

"Well, I don't know. Your ma needs lookin' after."

"I can do that, Sarah," Elizabeth offered. "I need to keep busy. The girls can clean up the kitchen, and I'll find some chores for the boys."

Ruth held her breath awaiting Sarah's answer.

"I do need to stop by the butcher. Feedin' this crowd has left the pantry a bit bare. Okay, that's the plan, then."

The morning meal complete, everyone left for their assigned chores. Cal and George were asleep, Sarah left to retrieve Cal's mother, Elizabeth, went upstairs to tend to the Squire's.

The girls were finally alone.

"We've got to leave soon before Cal and George wake up." Ruth set the glasses in the cupboard.

"How are we going to get out of the house dressed like floozies, Ruth?"

"We will have to dress somewhere else."

"Where?"

"I don't know. We'll have to get a cab, leave by the back door before anyone has a chance to miss us." Ruth hung up the dishtowel. "Come on, let's pack a bag with the clothes and get out of here. I'll get the cab to meet us down the block."

The house was quiet, no one was about. They hurried upstairs, threw the clothes into a bag, and were about to leave when Hattie whispered, "Wait." She gathered the rouge pots on Ruth's dresser, and a few other makeup items, and threw them in the bag.

They made it down the stairs and to the back door.

"Did you call the cab?"

Ruth opened the screen door. "Yes, now come on."

The alley was empty, and they ran the half block to the corner. A minute later, the cab pulled to the curb.

"Where to, ladies?"

Ruth was stumped. She hadn't thought that far ahead.

Hattie came to the rescue. "The fish market on Oak."

The cabbie glanced in his mirror. "That's a pretty rough part of town for the likes of you two. You sure you want to go there? I know another fish market in a nicer neighborhood."

"Look mister, I'm the new owner of the Whitewood Boarding House. The old owner said it is the only place she buys her seafood. If it's good enough for her, it's good enough for me."

"Right then, sorry miss."

Ruth ducked her head and whispered, "Fish market? We're going to change in a fish market?"

"It's the only place I know close to the docks. Mrs. Whitewood has been going there for years. She took me down there to meet the owner. "We'll figure it out when we get there."

The drive only took about fifteen minutes. Ruth paid the driver, grabbed the bag, and motioned for Hattie to hurry.

They stood on the curb until the cab was out of sight.

"Now what?" Ruth looked up at the Fish Market sign.

"Let's go in," Hattie suggested.

The smell of fish almost knocked them over, but once inside, the proprietor greeted them warmly.

"Ah, Miss Morgenstern, how good to see you today. All is well with Mrs. Whitewood, I hope?"

"Hello again, Mrs. Krämer, I was hoping you would be here. Mrs. Whitewood is fine. I'm here to ask a favor as the new proprietor of the boarding house." She turned to Ruth. "This is my friend, Ruth Squire. She is going to audition for a job as a singer, and well, her parents are not thrilled with the idea. I was hoping you would let her change into her costume in the back of your store."

The German woman frowned. "Going against your mama, little one?"

Ruth started to answer, but the woman cut her off.

"I was young and the dreamer once myself. Do you think I wanted to end up the wife of a fish monger?" She laughed, and her ample bosom shook with merriment. "Now, if my husband were here, he would send you packing, but as it turns out, he's not. The days are quite monotonous, as you may well imagine, here by the docks. Oh, we get the occasional murder, but for the most part, it's selling fish and visiting with the locals."

Ruth dared not breathe. It looked like the woman was going to help them out.

She looked Ruth up and down. "A singer, you say?"

"Yes, ma'am," Hattie answered.

"Well…there's a room in the back. You can change there. But if your parents come looking for ya, I'll have to tell them. I'm a mama myself. I would want to know."

The girls nodded and bolted for the room she pointed out.

Inside, they hurried to change. There was only a small cracked mirror hanging on the dingy wall, so it was hard to see the finished product.

Hattie inspected Ruth and applied the makeup.

In turn, Ruth made sure Hattie looked the part.

"How do we get out of here without her seeing us?" Ruth looked around.

"We'll have to go out the front. There is no choice but to trust her. It's our only chance." Hattie peeked through the crack in the door. The store was empty except for Mrs. Krämer. "Let's go."

"What about our other clothes?"

"We'll have to leave them here. Maybe we will live long enough to come back and get them." Hattie pushed Ruth through the door.

Mrs. Krämer's eyes grew big at the sight of them. "You too, Miss Hattie? You are wanting to be a singer, as well?"

"No, no, Mrs. Krämer. I am along as a chaperone, to make sure they don't take advantage of young Ruth. You see, I am dressing the part, so they believe she is a part of a company. You know how show business is —

it's not what you know, but who you know." Hattie nudged Ruth toward the door.

The German woman called after them, "She will be a new star, I can tell you that. Her beauty is breathtaking."

They both pulled their coats tight around them. The air was sharp and cold.

Outside, they ducked behind an old building.

"Why are you pushing me, Hattie?"

"We can't be seen like this, Ruth. If the police see us, they'll pick us up for, well…you get the picture."

"Oh, that wouldn't do, at all. Can we see The Blue Feather from here?" She craned her neck around the corner.

Hattie took a peek and pulled her back. "I think it's down a block or two. I heard Cal talking to George and Nick the other night. We'll go from building to building until we get close enough to walk in."

Ruth was so happy to have Hattie by her side. Her knees shook, and she couldn't get a clean breath for the fear pounding in her chest. She had talked a big game with Hattie, but now that they were here, reality punched her in the stomach.

Foot by foot, they shuffled from building to building, hiding in the alleyways. Luckily, the docks were quiet. It was mid-morning, and Ruth guessed the unsavory types were holed up waiting for the cover of night. *I only hope Peter is safe and asleep somewhere.*

Hattie jabbed her elbow into Ruth's ribs. "There it is. See the sign? It says The Blue Feather."

"I see it. This is it. Shall we go in?" Ruth looped her arm through Hattie's.

Hattie stood firm. "What if they only want one singer?"

"I can't stop now. We'll have to convince them we are a package deal. It's both of us or nothing." Ruth shivered and pulled her forward. "Come on."

Together, they walked toward the club, eyes forward, shoulder to shoulder until they stopped in front of the sign that read 'The Blue Feather'.

An Unlikely Beginning

Chapter Twenty-Seven

Zapelli closed the door behind the three working girls, put his foot on an empty chair, and leaned forward until he was almost nose to nose with Peter. "We got a little different cargo for the first run tonight, Kirby. These here dolls want to do a little 'shopping' over yonder, tonight. You got any objection to that?"

Peter closed he eyes, then opened them, again. "No, I've got no problem."

Zapelli leaned back. "Good." He moved his attention to Moose. "We've got a big cargo. The demand is growin'. I want more loads. Work 'em hard."

"Yes, boss."

"Girls, you come with me. Fanny'll fix you up until we leave, tonight. Moose, take these jokers upstairs. They're gonna need some rest. If they give ya any trouble, shoot 'em. Plenty more where they come from."

A knock on the door interrupted Moose's reply.

Zapelli jerked open the door. "What? It better be important for you to barge into my business meetin'."

Fanny stood at the door, both hands on her hips. "You plannin' to get rid of me, Giovanni? You could have at least come and talked to me."

"What are you yammerin' about? Why would I get rid of you? You're my sister."

Fanny inclined her head toward the main club room. "Two dames showed up. Said they were here for an audition. I'm the singer here, Giovanni. Everybody knows that."

Zapelli craned his neck to look into the club. "I don't know nothin' about no singers." He looked at Moose. "You doin' business behind my back?"

Moose paled. "No, boss. You know I wouldn't do that. I don't know nothin' about those dames."

"I'll check 'em out and get rid of 'em. Take Adams and Kirby upstairs."

Peter was glad for the distraction, but disappointed he wouldn't have a chance to check out the cabinet in the corner. *Maybe I'll have time to talk to Alexander about an escape plan.*

He tried to get a look at the women in the club, but Moose waved his gun toward the stairs as they came out of the meeting room. All he saw was a dark-haired girl in a blue dress.

Moose pushed them inside and locked the door. Peter waited until he heard Moose's footsteps thud down the stairs.

"Adams, we need to talk. Time is running out. We need a plan," Peter began.

"I don't know about you, Kirby, but I have an ace in the hole. Fanny's going to get me out of this mess."

Peter needed to plant the seed of doubt now. "Really, Adams? You trust her? From what I've seen, she's playing you. From what I can see, her eye is on Moose."

It worked. Adams smug smile shrank to a thin, grim line. "You're lying. You want me to help you escape.

It's not gonna work, Kirby. You're on your own." He turned his back.

Peter pushed harder. "Moose was up here earlier, to wake me. He was hopping mad, didn't like it you were downstairs flirting with Fanny—threatened to plug you, if the boss would let him."

Adams swiveled on one foot, mouth slack. "Are you telling me the truth?" Fear danced across his face, and his bottom lip quivered like a small child.

"Do you think I want to see you killed? They have no intentions of letting either one of us out of here alive. We need to work together." Peter went to the small, soot smeared window. "They might fit us with new shoes, Adams. The cement kind."

"But, Fanny said…"

"Fanny is a member of the mob family. She grew up in this atmosphere. When it comes right down to it, where do you think her loyalty lies?"

"She said she likes my manners, my refinement."

Peter laughed. "Manners can't buy her furs and jewels, Adams. I've seen the clothes she wears. Besides, you have a wife and daughter. They know that. They're using you."

Adams remained silent.

Peter lay across the bed with both hands behind his head. "If you want to try to work on an escape plan, let me know. I'll be over here thinking on how to save my own skin."

Fanny and her brother walked into the club together. Almost as an afterthought, he waved in her direction, and said, "Go cook somethin', Fanny. I'll take care of this."

"I want to…"

Zapelli glared. "I said go."

Ruth was struck by the man's huge nose. He was dressed perfectly, but his vocabulary was rough, uncouth.

"Now, ladies, what brings you to The Blue Feather?"

Hattie stepped forward. "We heard you are hiring singers. She sings."

He sat down in a chair, crossed his legs, took out a cigar, and lit it. "Where would you have heard such a thing?"

"It's on the street, everywhere," she continued.

"Is that so?" He puffed two long drags and exhaled three lazy, white rings.

"We want a shot to do something different. We're tired of singing in the church choir."

Ruth was stunned. Hattie played the part beautifully.

"Fanny does all the singin' here, girls." He looked them up and down…slowly.

The bile rose in Ruth's throat, but before she allowed it to get control, she stepped in front of Hattie. "Maybe you should hear us before you make a judgment. I'm sure Fanny is a fine singer, but it couldn't hurt to have a little variety."

The thought seemed to interest the mob boss. He pulled on the cigar and continued to look them over.

A few minutes transpired. Ruth thought he would send them on their way. Instead, he stood up.

"Moose," he called.

"Yeah, boss."

"Get the band over here."

"But boss, they always sleep this time of day. They gotta play all night long."

Zapelli never took his eyes off of the girls. "You arguin' with me, Moose?"

"No, boss, right away, boss. I'll go get them right now."

Zapelli walked around the girls while they stood in the middle of the floor. "So, you want an audition? Okay, I'll give ya one, but you better be good. It's not healthy to walk into this neighborhood uninvited, if you know what I mean. You two girls got guts."

"We just want to sing, Mr. ...?" Hattie said.

"Zapelli, the name is Giovanni Zapelli. My friends call me 'The Nose'. Maybe you've heard of me."

Ruth froze. Zapelli? That's the name of the man Sarah killed twenty years ago. What have I gotten myself into? If he finds out who I am, he'll kill me and Hattie, too.

"No, can't say that we have, Mr. Zapelli." Hattie moved in front of Ruth, protectively.

"Call me, Giovanni. If you work out, we could be real good friends." He smirked. "Sit down, take a load off. Those shoes gotta hurt your feet. The band will be along shortly. Why don't you tell me your names?" He went toward the bar. "Want something to drink?"

Ruth started to refuse, but Hattie elbowed her. "Yes, bourbon, if you have it. My name is Harriet, this is Ruby."

"Ah, a woman after my own heart. Well, Harriet, I've got the best bourbon this side of Canada." He laughed loud and long. "Two bourbons coming up."

Ruth whispered, "I don't drink, Hattie. I've never touched the stuff."

Hattie replied, "All I can say, is you better learn. Just don't choke."

With one eye on the girls, Zapelli slid two highball glasses across the counter, tipped his head toward Hattie, and said, "Drink up, ladies."

Ruth was acutely aware of the twisted grin on his face.

Hattie reached for the drink first, swirled it in the glass, sniffed it, and downed it in one gulp.

"Nice," said Zapelli.

The urge to gasp almost gave her away, but Ruth suppressed it. She must remember to ask Hattie where she learned to drink.

Now, it was her turn. She reached for the glass, but Hattie batted her hand away.

Zapelli flinched and reached for his pocket.

"You know you can't drink before you sing, Ruby. It tightens your vocal cords." She looked at Zapelli. "Do you any have lemon water?"

"Lemon water?"

"It's the only thing I let her drink before she sings," Hattie explained.

"Fanny!" he called.

She must have had her ear to the door because it burst open in a split second at the sound of her name. "Yes, Giovanni?"

"Get Ruby, here, some lemon water."

"What?"

"You heard me, lemon water."

Fanny retreated into the kitchen, and a couple of minutes later, emerged with a glass of water, and a slice of lemon stuck on the rim. She handed it to Zapelli.

"Okay, lemon water. Drink up," he said.

Ruth took the glass, took a sip, and offered a tentative smile to Fanny. "Thank you."

A commotion distracted the mob leader from his study of the two women. One by one, three men burst through the door, cussing and complaining.

"What's all the lip? Shut up and do what I pay ya for. These ladies want an audition. We're gonna give 'em one." Zapelli took out a match and flicked it between two fingers until it lit.

Ruth didn't know what the gesture meant, but all three men snapped to attention and hurried toward the bandstand to set up the instruments.

"Where's Mugsy?"

"He's comin' boss. His stomach was acting up." The trombone player hurried to get his horn out of its case.

"Well, he better…"

"I'm here, sorry boss."

Ruth couldn't help but notice the fear on each man's face. The one they called Mugsy looked green around the gills. It was obvious he wasn't feeling well. "Maybe we should come back, Mr. Zapelli. This doesn't look like a good time."

Hattie coughed. "Ruby, dear, you know we can't come back. We'll never be able to come back. It's now or never."

Zapelli sauntered over to the Ruth. "Getting' cold feet, doll?"

Ruth raised her voice to be heard over the noise of instruments warming up. "No, it's...he looks ill. I don't want to put them out any."

"He can be sick on his own time. I pay them to play music, and that's what they are gonna do."

Mugsy was at the piano. "Ready boss, what's the lady singin'?"

"Tell the man what your singin' doll."

Ruth walked to the bandstand and whispered in Mugsy's ear, "Do you know A Good Man Is Hard To Find?"

"Sure do. That's a mighty ambitious song for a little thing like you. Sure you can handle it?"

"Just play." She took a deep breath, gave Hattie a tremulous smile, and took her place on stage.

The piano man rolled out the introduction and nodded the cue to begin.

The first few notes came out breathy and weak. Her knees shook, but with Mugsy's vigorous nodding her voice strengthened, and by the time she reached the chorus, she was belting out the song as good as Marion Harris ever did.

She ventured a look at Hattie and almost laughed out loud at the shock registered on her face. However, she wasn't here to please her friend. Her gaze turned to Zapelli. A toothy grin spread across his face.

"Not bad, doll, not bad at all. We could use a looker like you around here." He pointed his cigar at Hattie. "What about you, Harriet was it? You sing, too?"

"Well, no, I handle Ruby, take care of her, make sure she eats right."

"I got no use for no deadbeats. You don't sing, I don't need ya." He looked away.

"If she goes, I go," Ruth said—her voice firm.

An audible gasp hung in the air like a death knell. Fanny had inched back into the bar when she heard Ruth sing.

The look on Zapelli's face could bring Capone to his knees. "You trying to tell me how to run my business, little lady?"

Hattie grabbed her arm. "Ruby, no…"

"I repeat—I need a handler. If she goes, we don't have a deal." Eyes fixed on his, she shrugged Hattie off.

An eerie quiet marked time, minute by minute. Ruth stared Zapelli down, not daring to even breathe.

An almost imperceptible chuckle broke the tension before he broke out into a full-blown laugh. "You got guts, doll."

"Well…do we have a deal or not? I don't need this job so bad I would leave her behind. There are other clubs." Deep inside, her heart palpitated in an erratic rhythm, but her eyes stayed riveted on his.

For the first time, he addressed his sister in the corner of the room. "What do ya say, Fanny? It might be good for business."

"I…I like her, Giovanni. She's got spunk, like me. I vote we keep her."

He looked surprised. "I figured you put the nix on it, sis. Okay, that's one vote. What about the rest of you."

Mugsy spoke up first. "I like her. We need some new blood in this place. Sorry, Fanny. No offense."

Only murmurs of agreement from the rest of band.

"Looks like you got the job, but I got rules. You already broke one of them. She stays, but you do things my way, understand? There's a room upstairs. You two will share it. If I pay your wages, you live here, where I can keep an eye on ya." He took a long drag on the cigar. "Kapeesh?"

Both women nodded.

"Fanny, show 'em where they bunk." The cigar made a plunk sound in the brass spittoon as he flicked it aside. "You go on at ten, be ready."

Ruth and Hattie grabbed hands and followed Fanny up the stairs. At the landing, Ruth heard voices in one of the rooms, they were male voices, and her heart skipped a beat. Could it be Peter?

Hattie must have heard them, as well, by the wide-eyed glance she threw her way. Neither woman spoke, only followed the hostess into the room at the end of the hall.

Inside, Fanny took charge. "There are two bunks. It don't matter who sleeps where. You got any clothes?" When they replied no, Fanny continued, "Well, we got plenty. You'll find 'em in the closet." She stopped long enough to give Ruth the once over. "That outfit will do for tonight, but you'll have to wear somethin' with a little more oomph next time."

She started out of the room, but turned back. "Dinner's at eight. Be on time or there won't be any." The door closed with a bang.

"Oomph?" Ruth repeated. "What does that mean exactly?"

Hattie flung open the closet doors. "We can probably find oomph in here." A long, low whistle eased across her lips. "Would you look at this?"

"I don't want to look. Fanny said this would be fine for tonight. I don't plan on being here any longer. After we find Peter, we leave."

Hattie closed the door. "Listen, Ruth. Don't get it in your head we're going to get out of this place tonight. These guys are not nice people. Just because you got away with outsmarting the boss today, doesn't mean he'll let you walk out of here."

The bed sagged under her weight. "Don't talk about it, Hattie. My heart is still pounding. It came out of my mouth before I could stop myself." A silent shudder danced down her spine. "Where did that come from? I know I'm headstrong, but he might have told those goons to kill us."

Hattie chuckled. "I have a good idea your momma had that kind of spunk as a girl. The truth of the matter is you are in love. Peter is in danger and your desire to protect him kicked in."

"Well, maybe, or it could be I am immature and stupid." Ruth debated on whether to tell her friend about the long standing connection she had with Zapelli, but under the circumstances decided Hattie's knowing would put her more at risk.

The bedsprings groaned even more at the arrival of Hattie beside Ruth. "Hardly stupid, more like crazy in love."

"Wait...listen, Hattie." She stood. "Do you hear that?"

"Those voices? Yes, I heard them on the way up the stairs."

"They are louder. Do you think it's Peter?"

"Try the lock," Hattie whispered.

The air in the room now turned close, almost stifling. Their eyes locked. Ruth was the first to turn away and walk to the door.

The doorknob was grimy and loose fitting in the socket. She gripped tightly and twisted.

Chapter Twenty-Eight

Cal Taylor woke with a start. The room was still light, so he knew time actually spent asleep was short. He hoped to get a restful sleep, but the need to form a plan for Peter's rescue invaded his sub consciousness. However, there was something else, a haunting awareness…apprehension.

A knock on the door made him sit upright. "Come in."

Sarah poked her head into the room, but didn't step inside. "Master Cal, I hate botherin' you, but I'm gettin' a mite worried. When I got back from fetchin' your ma, the girls were gone. I figured they went to the market, but it's been hours, now, and they have yet to return."

"Both of them?" The air in the room turned colder and not for lack of a fire in the hearth.

"Yes sir," Sarah replied.

"Two headstrong women—Lord only knows what they've cooked up between them." He shouldered past Sarah. "Have you looked everywhere, asked Ruth's parents, my mother?"

"That would be the first thing I did, sir. Sure didn't want to bother your rest. Too much time has passed. Do you think someone took 'em?"

It wasn't beyond the stretch of reason to think someone hijacked them, just like Peter, but for some reason, Cal knew different. "No, no, Sarah, I don't think anyone took them. When those two make up their minds about something, it usually comes to pass. My first guess is they went down to the docks."

Sarah gasped. "The docks? Why, they could get in a world of trouble down there. The thought never crossed my mind. I've wasted so much time. They could be hurt, or worse."

Cal grabbed Sarah's shoulders. "It's not your fault, Sarah. The girls must have cooked up a plan. I'll get George and head down there. I was hoping for the cover of night."

"I should go with you, Master Cal. They might need me."

"No, and don't tell a soul about this. There is enough worry to go around. It could be they went to the police station. We won't jump to conclusions before we know more." He released her and bolted down the stairs. George wouldn't be happy about the abrupt change of plans, but he had no choice now.

George grumbled at Cal's insistent shaking. "Why in the devil are you waking me up at this time of day. It won't be dark for hours."

The curtains rasped against the rods as Cal pushed them open to let in the light. "The girls are missing. They could be in trouble."

"Girls? What girls?" George sat up and rubbed the stubble on his chin, blinking at the brightness in the room.

"Hattie and Ruth. Come on, they could be down at the docks. We've got to find them before someone else does." Cal hurried to the door. "Let's go."

"Whoa, now, Cal. What makes you think they are crazy enough to go down there? Could be they went shopping." George stumbled to follow.

"We're talking Hattie and Ruth, here, George. Peter is missing, you dolt. Ruth wouldn't go shopping at a time like this. If Ruth hatched a plan, she drew Hattie into it."

Sarah was in the kitchen pouring hot steaming coffee. "Here, you'll need this to getcha goin'."

Cal grabbed the mug and gulped quickly. "Thanks Sarah, you always know what to do."

George continued to grumble. "I don't see why we have to go down there in broad daylight. Can't we get the coppers involved?"

"They haven't done anything about Peter, what makes you think they would do anything about the girls?" He stopped in the doorway. "Remember Sarah, say nothing to anyone. I'll get word to you as quick as I can."

She nodded.

The day was fading, but out in the open air, life ticked along as it did every day. People walked up and down the sidewalks, automobiles motored toward their various destinations, everyone busy with their own lives as if nothing out of the ordinary had happened. Cal even saw the substitute milk driver turning a corner on Peter's route. It gave him a twinge, and he peered closer…to make sure it wasn't really Peter. No one would miss Peter for a while, no one had any notion of the danger in the city.

As they drove toward the docks, George kept looking over at Cal. "You got a problem, George? Am I driving too fast for you?"

"No, I'm wondering what kind of hair brained scheme you've got up your sleeve. It'd be nice to have a plan."

The road was bumpy; he kept his eyes forward. "I've got a plan. Don't worry."

George slapped his cap on his knee. "Well wouldn't it be nice if you let me in on it?"

"Have I ever let you down in all these years? Trust me; you know I fly by the seat of my pants, George. Things come clear to me when the adrenaline kicks in."

"Yeah, it gives me real comfort, Cal." He slid down in the seat and crossed his arms in a pout.

The boardwalk looked almost empty as they drew close. He decided to park where he had before. They would have to take their chances on foot.

A quick look around to scout possible routes for escape, and he breathed a little easy. Several markets were open—the bakery, the butcher shop, and the fish market. He supposed they did a fair business during the day, but was sure they closed up tight at night when the action began. One possibility was they paid the mob for protection. Even so, they might be possible escape routes if things got dicey.

Cal turned his collar up against the brisk wind, motioned for George to follow, and trudged toward the first shop.

"I think I'll ask if they've seen the girls." He didn't wait for his partner's response.

Inside the bakery, he asked if the owner's had seen two women and described them. The workers only shook their heads.

At the butcher shop, the proprietor was anxious for them to leave, and said he had seen nothing.

Finally, Cal decided to try the fish market. "Have you seen two women...young, one tall, one a bit shorter, black hair?"

The woman eyed them suspiciously. "Who wants to know?"

"One of the women is my business partner. She buys fish down here sometimes. She bought the boarding house from Mrs. Whitewood. Surely, you know her. There is something urgent happening at home and I wanted her to know about it. The other woman is a bit younger, shiny black hair, about so tall." He held his hand to about his chin.

A few seconds of silence gave Cal hope.

"Ain't seen nothin' all day. Sorry." She turned around and started to wrap two large fish in butcher paper.

"You're sure?" Cal asked.

The woman didn't look up or turn around. "I'm sure. Now, if you don't mind, I'm busy with an order."

Cal's shoulders slumped. He could have sworn the woman was about to tell him something.

"Did it seem to you she knew more than she was saying?" Cal addressed George outside the shop.

"Beats me. I think your imagination is running away, Cal. This thing with Peter has got you jumpy. I say let's stick with the plan and come back tonight. It's too dangerous in the daytime."

"You can go anytime you want, George. I'm not forcing you to come with me. It's not like the girls to disappear for hours, especially when they are waiting for news of Peter. No, they are up to something, and I am going to find out what." He walked briskly toward the docks.

Cal could hear the footsteps behind him and smiled. George wouldn't let him down; the guy was faithful to the end, even though he complained.

He decided to cross the street and not walk directly in front of the Blue Feather. If he was stopped for any reason, he would say he was looking for someone.

A few more steps, and they were directly across the street from the infamous club. It was quiet, no one around.

"Now what?" George whispered from behind.

A narrow alley separated two buildings on that side of the street. "We duck in here and wait."

The doorknob caught—locked.

Hattie cursed. "Better step away, Ruth. You never know who might be on the other side, lurking."

It looked to be about five o'clock by the sun through the window. Hours before she would have to perform. Ruth only knew a couple of songs by heart and hoped it would be enough. The possibility Peter was near gave her comfort. She sat beside Hattie and took her hand. "I hope I can do this, Hattie. It's beginning to hit me…what I've gotten us into. I'm sorry. You shouldn't be here; it's my problem, not yours. When Cal finds out he'll be furious with me."

230

"Nonsense, I have a mind of my own. How could I rest knowing you were out here by yourself with no one to watch your back? Fanny will be back in a couple of hours. Maybe she'll let us come down to dinner. We can scout around for any sign of Peter, then. Better get some rest."

Hattie pulled the cracked, yellowed blind over the small window and settled into the dingy overstuffed chair in the corner.

"There is plenty of room on the bed," Ruth said.

"You need to rest without me bouncing around. Stage time will come soon enough. We're not going anywhere, so may as well accept it until Fanny comes back."

A sudden pounding on the door made them both jump to their feet.

"You dames decent?" Moose's voice bellowed on the other side. "The boss wants to see ya."

An Unlikely Beginning

Chapter Twenty-Nine

The door down the hall closed with a bang. Peter opened one eye. *I wonder who else Zapelli has stashed up here.*

Captain Alexander Adams sat in the corner of the room apparently deep in thought, hands folded over both knees, eyes staring at the door.

"Wonder who's out there, Adams? Maybe 'The Nose' getting tired of us, ready to dump us in the drink."

The Captain never flinched, the sockets of his eyes hollow, as if he'd been staring at the door all afternoon. "I thought you were asleep."

"Nope, not asleep. I've been thinking of a plan to escape once we get out on the docks tonight. What about you?" Peter stood and stretched his hands to the ceiling. "I'm getting kind of hungry. Wonder what Fanny fixed for dinner?"

Still as a statue, Adams whispered, "Do you really think Fanny is using me to get at Moose?"

A twinge of guilt trifled with his conscience, but Peter figured it was his only chance to get Adams on his side and ultimately escape. "I wouldn't have said anything if I didn't see it for the truth."

Finally, Adams shifted his gaze to Peter. "Then, we need to think of a plan to escape."

"That is what I have been telling you. We need to do it tonight, before the last shipment. Are you sure you're in?"

"I'm sure. There is my wife and daughter to consider. Fanny is only a passing fancy…like Priscilla, but my whole life is my station in the community where I live. I couldn't disgrace them…my wife, my daughter, my mother." Adams looked as though he would cry.

A surge of anger coursed through Peter's body. *So all the suffering Priscilla Squire and her family endured was only a passing fancy to the good Captain. I thought as much.* He clenched and unclenched his fists, but maintained his composure. "What about your father? You didn't mention him."

Adams leaped out of the chair, face flushed, eyes glowing. "My father can be hanged. He is the one who forced me into the situation of marriage. I wasn't ready. However, after years of enjoying a certain life style, I know I cannot live without it."

"Whoa, settle down, Captain. I wasn't judging you, only making an observation." Peter backed away.

The Captain eased backwards and plopped back down on the chair. "Sorry, he still riles me."

"Listen—hear that? Is that Moose's footsteps I hear? I wonder if he is coming to get us for supper." Peter watched the doorknob to see if it would turn.

It didn't, but the footsteps continued down the hall to the next room.

Peter heard Moose say something about 'dames'. A couple of minutes later, he heard the soft whisper of women's voices pass the door and follow Moose downstairs. "Well, it doesn't look like they are coming for us, does it? I suppose those are ladies of a particular 'class' he's got stored away up here. They might be our cargo for the evening."

Adams ignored the door and stared at Peter. "How can you be so calm through all of this? I am terrified. What is your plan? I'm on your side, now. I want to get out of here."

Peter took the chair and motioned for Adams to take the bed. "If you're sure I can count on you, I'll share the plan, but you have to follow it to the letter. Okay?"

Captain Adams hurried to the bed, sat down, and nodded his head. "Anything you say, Kirby. I'll do anything; only get me out of here."

"Alright, first thing we're going to do is get into the kitchen some way. You have to distract Fanny, tease her, flattery, anything to get her to let you into the kitchen. When you are in, you get close to a drawer, pretend to kiss her, lean her against the counter. Do what you do, lover boy. Ease a drawer open and extract a knife, stuff it into your pocket, and keep it hidden until we are out on the boat. Once on the water…

Moose practically kicked open Zapelli's door and pushed the girls inside. "Here they are boss, just like you said."

"Good work, Moose, now make yourself scarce. Go put a prod to Fanny and get these people fed. There's gonna be an early crowd tonight. Havin' a special guest." Zapelli waved the ever-present cigar at the big thug. "So girls, get a good rest? I want you to eat your

235

grub now, so's it will digest and all before your big debut."

Hattie spoke first, "Exactly what is for dinner, Mr. Zapelli? Ruby must be careful what and how much she eats before a performance. Wouldn't want to weigh her down, you see."

The giggles, despite the serious situation, threatened to surface. Hattie played the part to perfection. Ruth forced her thoughts back to Peter and his need of rescue. "Yes, Mr. Zapelli, I have to be careful of my voice."

He stood, brushed a stack of papers off his desk, and snapped, "Would ya quit callin' me Mr. Zapelli! The name is Giovanni, and that's what I want you to call me. Giovanni, got it?"

Ruth jumped. "Sure, Mr...I mean Giovanni, whatever you want. We were only trying to be respectful, you being the boss and all." She caught the fear on Hattie's face. Maybe she wasn't as strong willed as she supposed.

The air apparently went out of Zapelli's sails, because he sat down and fashioned a sheepish smile on his face. "Hey, I didn't mean to yell." The cigar twirled in one hand, a habit he evidently couldn't break. "You see, I've been thinkin'. I like you Ruby. You got a different look about ya. Not like the other dames around this place. Maybe you'd want to be my special girl, huh? Whaddya say?"

The blood in Ruth's veins turned to ice, and she thought her heart would stop. She stammered, took a step back, felt Hattie's hand on her waist, but before she could form an answer, the door burst open.

"Hey boss, there's a couple of mugs lurkin' out in the alley across the street. I thought you oughta know." It was Moose. Big, burly, clumsy, stupid, Moose.

Ruth was never so glad to see anyone in all her life.

Zapelli took the revolver out of the holster under his jacket, cocked it, and pointed it right at Moose's head. "Whaddya mean come bustin' in here. Can't you see I'm in the middle of somethin'?"

Moose's face blanched marble white. He sputtered something unintelligible and started to back out of the door, hands in front of his face. For a moment, he looked like the little boy that lurked inside of the big galoot.

"Wait a minute. Where ya goin'? I didn't say you could leave." Zapelli got up, walked to the window, and looked outside. "I don't see nothin'."

"They ducked inside the alley. I seen 'em plain as day." Moose dropped his hands and stepped back into the room.

Now, Ruth's heart thudded with fear. Oh, please don't tell me Cal is here. She glanced at Hattie and could tell she was thinking the same thing.

Suddenly, Zapelli whirled and grabbed Ruth by the arm, twisting it behind her back. "You expectin' somebody?" He dragged her toward the window and forced her to look out. "This better not be a set-up, doll."

Her heart still hammered in her chest, but she was determined to maintain calm. Their lives depended on it. In a calm voice that belied the adrenaline pumping in her veins, she said, "I told you my story, Giovanni. There is no one who would follow me. I wanted out; I wanted excitement, show business. Whoever's out there is no friend of mine."

For some unknown reason, Zapelli released her and jostled her lightly toward Hattie. "You better not be lyin' to me. I've put dames at the bottom of the river before. I ain't choosy."

"Look boss, there they are, inside the alleyway. Do ya think they are casin' the joint? Could be somebody from the Kirby gang, looking for ole Pete upstairs." Moose's confidence oozed.

Zapelli reached out and slapped Moose alongside the head. "Ain't you got no sense? Don't be spreadin' our business around." He grabbed Ruth's arm again and drew her close to him." Tell ya what I'm gonna do." This time he looked at Hattie. "Miss Harriet here is goin' out there and talk to the fellas. I'm gonna keep the little songbird here with me. If I see one thing out of the ordinary, Ruby here gets it."

Hattie's hand flew to her throat. "Me? Why not send Moose? What can I do if they get edgy?"

"You heard what I said. Moose will escort you to the door like a proper gentleman. I'll know in an instant if they recognize you, so don't try any funny business." He squeezed Ruth's arm tighter.

She hoped her eyes conveyed the message she so badly wanted to shout out to Hattie, but knew she couldn't. The only comfort, at this point, was that Hattie was good on her feet, strong, smart. She knew the score. Cal, surely, would know it's a trap and play along. Please God.

Moose, seemingly recovered from fear, shoved Hattie in front of him and toward the main door. "Let's go, chickadee. Let's find out who these jokers are."

Zapelli and Ruth watched through the window.

Hattie emerged from the club and stood on the sidewalk.

Ruth's heart stopped, she couldn't breathe. Would Cal come running toward her, give them away, put all of them in jeopardy?

Nothing moved. No one came out of the alley. The alleyway was too dark to see if anyone was in there or not. Hattie looked back at Moose. He said something to her, but Ruth couldn't hear what. She nodded and took a few steps toward the road. Step by step, she crossed the street, stopping to look back at Moose, until she finally made it across.

Ruth and Zapelli couldn't see into the alleyway from the window, but Moose could. One word from him...and Ruth could be dead. She crossed her fingers, prayed silently, and waited. As she dared to breathe, without warning, Hattie stepped into the alley and disappeared.

Cal couldn't believe his eyes. He was about to tell George they should leave, when out of the club walked Hattie. At least, he thought it was her; it was hard to tell by the getup she wore. Not one day since he'd known her had he ever seen her dressed in red. Conservative, sensible, strong, with good moral values—that was the girl he knew. Not this...this...well, he didn't know what to call her.

239

Heavy makeup, hair twisted up, feathers. It wasn't her, it couldn't be her. Yet, as she drew closer, he recognized the walk, the tilt of her head, those high cheek bones, and ruby lips. He whispered close to George's ear. "What in the name of anything sensible is she doing?"

"Let's get her in here and find out," George replied.

Cal nudged him hard. "No, they've got guns on her, I just know it. We have to behave like we don't know her. They must have spotted us." He looked behind her, tried to focus on the dark windows of the club. "Where is Ruth? I know she's with her."

Hattie stepped into the shadows. "Cal?" she called in a soft voice.

"Here," Cal whispered.

"They've got a gun on me, Cal. They will shoot Ruthie if they think we know each other. Please don't give it away."

"I figured as much." A plan began to form. "Step back into the sunlight. Shout at me; wave your hands. Act like I was just after girls, women, you know, get mad like I know you can. George and I will run out the back way. I'll be back tonight when it's dark. Please be careful." He paused. "Have you seen Peter?"

"No, but we heard voices in the next room. Male. Could be him."

"Okay, go, go!"

He listened while Hattie shouted into the alley. "You pervert. Get away from here. There are no girls like that around here. How dare you insult me in such a manner."

Cal pulled George after him and ran to the end of the alley. Hattie's voice faded, but he heard the expletives spouting from her mouth, and he smiled. "She's a good actress, George. I'll have to remember that."

They ran two blocks toward town to the automobile. No one followed, and Cal breathed easier.

"Are you going to leave her there, Cal?"

"We have no choice at the moment. You heard what she said, they have guns on them. Ruth is the hostage. Tonight—we go back tonight. Hattie sounded convincing. I only hope they buy it. All we can do is pray, at this point, and hope the girls use their wits."

A dozen scenario's rambled through his brain. The plan had to be perfect, because now he had to rescue Hattie and Ruth, as well as Peter.

"Cal?"

"What, George?"

"We can't go back to the house without the girls. Sarah will be fit to be tied. The whole house will be up in arms. Is it smart to upset the whole household? It'll be dark soon; maybe we should lay low until we can go back." George slung his arm across the back of the seat and turned to face Cal.

"Good idea, George. Where? We don't know if those mugs are looking for us. You know to be safe." Cal glanced around.

"Why not the boarding house? No one is there now, except old Mrs. Whitewood." George offered.

"Good thinking, Georgy boy. Now I know why I keep you around." The automobile swung hard to the left, and they sped toward Whitewood's Boarding House.

Ruth could hear Hattie shouting angrily into the alleyway, her hands waved violently in the air, and she stomped her foot. "Perverts! How dare you say such things. Yeah, you better run. My boys got guns pointed at your backs." She stopped, and then hollered a bit more. Finally, she turned around and walked briskly back to the club.

Zapelli forced Ruth to the open door of the office and watched Moose pull Hattie inside.

Moose slapped her on the back. "Mighty fine scolding, Ms. Harriet. I'd hate to be on your bad side. Didn't know 'em, huh?"

Hattie kept her head down and hurried toward Ruth. "A couple of young boys, looking for some thrills — thought I was some floozy."

The mob boss shoved Ruth into a chair and pointed for Hattie to take a seat, also. "Boys? You sure of that? 'Cause if I find out different, you'll be makin' new friends at the bottom of that river out there."

Ruth bolted from the chair. "Leave her alone, Zapelli. She did what you told her. Can't you see she's scared to death?"

Zapelli pushed her hard. She lost her balance and plopped back into the teetering chair. "When you gonna learn I call the shots around here? Nobody talks to me like that. You've crossed the line twice, missy, I'm not inclined to give you a stab at a third." He drew the pistol again, cocked it, and pointed it at her head.

Ruth didn't flinch. Something rose inside her, strength of will, a renewed defiance. Suddenly, all the confusion that rattled around in her mind fell into place. Like a jigsaw puzzle solved. All the pieces fit. Fear didn't consume her, instead a peaceful calm. She knew who she was now, and this pipsqueak wasn't going to take anything away from her.

With a slow deliberate movement, she pushed up from the chair until she stood eye level with this over-rated buffoon. He talked a good game, had his men in mortal fear of him, but his eyes revealed a different story. Never in a million years could he shoot a woman. In fact, she wondered if he had ever shot anyone.

Her voice was low, calm, even, and matched his threatening tone. "If you lay one hand on either Hattie or me, I will peel the skin from your grubby eyelids and make you eat it."

She stood perfectly still, hardly breathing, unblinking.

At first, his eyes widened in shock, but as the mob leader and the so called songbird stared each other down, those same orbs returned to normal size, and the light in them noticeably dimmed.

The room assumed a hushed tone. Hattie and Moose gaped in disbelief. The minutes ticked by in, almost painful, sixty second increments, the gun still directed at Ruth.

Fanny burst into the room. "Giovanni, you put that gun away right now. You ain't goin' down for killin' a woman."

An Unlikely Beginning

The gun clattered to the floor, a shot rang out, the women screamed. A grunt, a chair crashed against the wall, and drops of blood splattered the floor.

Chapter Thirty

Peter heard the shot, leapt from the bed, and hurried to the door.

Adams followed in similar fashion. "Was that a gunshot?"

"Sounded like it. Things must have gone wrong downstairs. I hope it wasn't the women. Even that type doesn't deserve an end like that." Peter rattled the door. "We've got to get out of here. We might be next."

The captain whirled Peter around. "I can't die like this, in a seedy room in a bar. Get me out of here, Kirby."

"Get control of yourself. I can't help you, if you don't help me." He shrugged off Adams grip. "Let's get this door open. Put your shoulder to it, man."

They were about to ram the door when footsteps crashed up the stairs, the lock in the door rattled, and the door opened wide.

Fanny stood there, breathing hard, sweat beading her brow, blood smeared on her hands. "Either one of you know how to dress a wound?"

Peter looked at Adams. "Surely, you had training in the Navy."

Fanny didn't wait for his answer; she grabbed the captain and pushed him out the door. "Come with us, Kirby, you might have to hold him down."

The scene in the downstairs office looked as if a bloody shootout took place. Moose lay on the floor crying like a baby, his shoulder running blood. Even Peter could see it was a flesh wound.

Fanny shoved Adams toward the big gangster. "You fix him. Stop the bleeding. If you don't I'll plug ya."

Peter watched, fascinated as Fanny pulled a gun from a holster strapped to her leg. He never would have guessed she carried such a weapon under her dress.

Adams blanched. "But, Fanny…I thought…"

"I'm not interested in what you think, Adams. Do as I say." She jerked the gun toward him.

Peter hurried to his side. "Let me help you, Captain." He reached under his jacket and tore the hem of his shirt into a long strip. "Tie this around the shoulder, it'll stop the bleeding. We need pressure."

The befuddled Navy officer looked at Peter, mouth slack.

"Go on, do it," Peter urged.

His mouth snapped shut and Adams snatched the makeshift bandage from Peter. Two swift movements, and the bandage was in place.

"Water," Peter barked. "He needs water."

Fanny turned around. "Mac, get some water from the kitchen. Be quick."

A pause in the action gave Peter a chance to look around the room. Giovanni Zapelli cowered in a corner, pale— eyes glazed. He was the only other person in the room.

Peter took a chance. "I thought I heard a woman's voice down here."

Fanny kept her eyes on Moose. "They're in the kitchen. Mac hustled them in there when the gun went off." For a split second, she glanced at Peter. "You mind your business. I ain't opposed to pullin' this trigger."

"Sorry, I was afraid one of them got hurt."

"Everything is under control, don't you worry. Fanny has it all under control," she whispered down at Moose.

The injured hit man stopped crying and looked up at her, eyes soft, filled with tears. "Oh, Fanny…"

In a flash, her face resumed a hardened expression. "Don't get all soft on me, Moose. We have an operation to run." As if for the first time, she looked at her brother hovering in the corner. "You sorry piece of…"

The mob boss didn't react, only maintained the panicked look in his eyes.

She dismissed him with a wave of the gun and barked an order. "Get Moose upstairs. One of you gets to take the bullet out."

Peter raised both hands in the air. "May I, Fanny?"

"May you what, Kirby? What are you babbling about?"

He motioned toward the wall. "I don't think the bullet is in his arm. It seems to be stuck in the wall."

She cast a warning glance at him and examined the wall. "You might be right."

Mac hurried into the room with a glass of water.

"You got a pen knife, Mac? Dig that bullet out of the wall."

"Yea, sure, I got a knife." Mac pulled it out of his pocket and did as he was told.

"Let's get him upstairs, Captain. We can examine the wound up there. I can tell if it really went through his shoulder or not. My guess is—that's the bullet in the wall...unless you make a habit of shooting people in this office."

Fanny cocked the gun. "Anymore lip out of you, Kirby, and I'll do what I promised. Get Moose up the stairs."

A certain awareness began to dawn on Peter. The look of shock on Giovanni's face, the way Fanny had total command of the situation and the gun, the way she barked orders like she had done it all her life. The picture emerged in his mind. Giovanni wasn't the true boss of this operation. Fanny was.

The men struggled to carry Moose up the stairs. The big lug weighed more than both of them—all muscle. Moose cursed and swore all the way up to the room.

Finally, they had him situated on the rickety bed. Adams lifted his head and got him to swallow some water.

Peter removed the bandage enough to see the wound. The hole went through the shoulder. "There is no bullet in his shoulder. It went all the way through. He'll be right as rain if he doesn't get an infection. We need some alcohol."

Fanny gave Mac instructions and watched as he left to do her bidding. "You two will stay here and doctor him. I gotta show to put on. No funny business. I still have plenty of men to carry your corpses down to the river."

Peter heard the click of the lock behind her retreat, and his heart sank. "There goes my plan to escape tonight at the river. We're stuck in here with this big galoot.

"She's in love with him. All this time, I thought she liked my manners, my refinement. She just used me." Adams stared down at Moose.

"We have more things to worry about than your love life, Adams. The door is locked. Do you get it? There is no escape plan." He shook him by the shoulders.

The light slowly dawned in Adams' eyes. "You mean we aren't going down to the river, tonight? We aren't going to escape?"

"How can we? The door is locked. They want us to doctor him." He turned away. "I should have let you flounder down there. I should have let you save your own skin. Now, I'm stuck in here with you." His fists clenched. "This is all your fault, Adams. I wouldn't be anywhere near here, if it weren't for you." He whirled and threw a wild punch at the startled captain.

Ruth and Hattie sat close together at the kitchen table. One of the mob's henchman stood guard.

The swinging door banged open, and Fanny burst in. "Your supper is in the warming oven. Eat and get up stairs. There is a show in an hour. You need to be ready."

"A show…you expect me to sing after what happened?" Ruth asked.

Fanny still had the gun in her hand.

Hattie reached out to quiet Ruth. "One shooting is enough for me, Ruthie. Let's go ahead and do what she says."

"Good advice, Harriet." She looked directly at Ruth. "This one's a little firecracker alright. Good thing you are here to calm her down." She turned on her heel and left.

The guard motioned for the women to get their meals out of the oven.

While they ate, Ruth whispered to her partner. "I wonder if he's dead."

"It was a shoulder wound. I doubt it killed him. He'll be out of commission for a few days." Hattie buttered a piece of bread and handed it to Ruth.

"I never expected all this, Hattie. Someone got shot. This is crazy."

"May I remind you, it was your idea?"

The rest of the meal was eaten in silence. After they finished, the gunman pointed the gun at them. "Upstairs til the show," he growled.

On the way down the hall, Ruth noticed the door of the next room stood wide open. No one was inside. I missed seeing who was in there. Will I ever find Peter?

Hattie tried to fix Ruth's makeup and brush her hair. "We're in this now, Ruthie. The game is on, and we have to play it. It could mean our lives and Peter's. Remember, Cal knows now. He'll think of something. We'll get out of this. You need to sing, convince them we are legitimate. If you don't play now, all of this will be in vain."

It was dark outside; they sat in the bedroom huddled on the bed, waiting for show time, too numbed to even turn on the light.

Eventually, the knock came. It was time.

In the far corner of the seedy speakeasy, Ruth tried to avoid the interested eye of a repugnant patron. The impatient bartender waved his hand toward the stage—it was her turn to sing, but the metallic taste of fear drenched her tongue and slithered downward until her stomach burned. She took a step back.

Hattie whispered from behind, "Remember why we are doing this Ruthie. You can't abandon him now."

Slowly, courage overtook the fear. One step—another, until she stood center stage. The piano man began the prelude, and she closed her eyes. A few tremulous notes exhaled through dry lips, but strengthened as memories of the murderous carnage at home played like a movie through her mind, and steeled her will. The choice to save him was hers. Instead of a pack of crude, bawdy men in a smoke filled room, she focused on Peter.

She belted out the same song she performed for Giovanni Zapelli and tried to filter out the catcalls and whistles. The smoke in the room clogged her throat until she could hardly breathe. When it was over, the applause was thunderous, they were calling for more.

Mugsy nodded at her. She walked over and whispered in his ear. He gave his band a few instructions, and once more, she sang another song she liked to practice in her room, alone. The reaction was the same, wild applause, catcalls, whistles. Panic

251

gripped her. She really didn't know the words to any other songs by heart. What would she do next?

To her great relief, Fanny came to her rescue. It was her turn to sing.

Fanny whispered in her ear as she passed Ruth on the way off the stage. "You done good, kid. Too good."

Ruth repeated Fanny's barb to Hattie. "What did she mean by that? Was I too good? I was scared to death."

Hattie snaked one arm around Ruth's waist and held her tight. "Ruthie, you are a natural. I had no idea you could sing like that. It's possible you made Fanny mad. She's the star of the show, you know, until now. Maybe you should botch the next song, make them boo you."

"Yea — and that might get us shot."

They paused to listen to Fanny's performance. She was good, no doubt about it. There was a good applause, but no catcalls, no whistles. Fanny all but stomped off the stage.

"Looks like it's you they want, tonight, Ruby." She brushed past her and off stage.

The stomping and pounding started out in the club. "Ruby, Ruby, Ruby." The men chanted.

"What should I do?"

"Ask Mugsy. He'll know." Hattie gave her a little push.

Hesitating only a second, she went on stage and looked at the piano player. "I don't know any more songs by heart, Mugsy."

"Can you read music?" he started to shuffle through some sheet music.

"Sure, I play a little piano, too. My mother made me take lessons."

"Good, here take this, there's a stand over there. Put it on the stand and follow my lead. Tell 'em your learnin' a new song, and you want to try it out on them. Fanny does it all the time. Do the best you can do with it. Put a little girly stuff in it, ya know, smile, bat your eyes. Give 'em what they came for." He shoved the music in her hand.

She took the sheet from him and walked over to the music stand, arranged it to her satisfaction, and looked out into the audience. It was hard to distinguish faces for the smoke that filled the room, but she could see a few rough looking characters, grinning toothless grins, fingers stuck in their mouths trying to whistle. A shudder ran down her spine, but she shrugged it off. "Thank you all for the warm welcome. If you will bear with me, I am new here and am learning a new song. Would you mind if I practiced on you?" She attempted a smile.

"We didn't come to hear you sing, lady!" One man hollered.

Raucous laughter filled the room.

She felt the blush spread up her neck and over her entire face. Mugsy rescued her by playing the opening score.

With her focus on the music, she began to sing the opening lines. The song was familiar, so she picked it up rather quickly.

In the middle of her rendition, there was a scuffle at the side of the stage. Two men being hustled down the stairs, a gunman behind them. She could see the glint of the weapon in his hand, pointed at the backs of the men. The distraction knocked her off guard and she tried to refocus, but then, recognition dawned. Peter!

At the same time, Peter looked directly at her. She could tell he didn't recognize her at first, but as he continued to descend the stairs, he looked at her again...and then, again. His eyes lit up, only to be replaced by a look of horror.

She spun around, her back to him. What must he think? The look on his face...

The crowd began to get restless, and Mugsy started the chorus again when she didn't pick it up.

The words came out of her mouth, the notes shrill, and off key. Boo's started to crop up around the room. She quickly recovered and got back on track. When she looked again, Peter was gone. Suddenly, there was no plan, no resolution—no escape. Once more, she acted impulsively, and this time, put all of them in peril. What had she been thinking, coming here...putting them all in danger?

A forced smile was all she could muster to appease the crowd. One by one, they settled down as the song progressed, and she put a little more effort into it. Her heart was wrenched at the site of Peter, a gun at his back. Were they going to take him out and shoot him? What should she do?

All of a sudden, police whistles pierced the air, officers shouted, "This is a raid!" A mad scramble ensued as patrons tried to escape the club without being caught.

Ruth was frozen to the spot. Mugsy and the band made their escape out the back way, leaving her there to fend for herself. Hattie ran out and grabbed her.

As her friend pulled her off stage, she saw Fanny in the small alcove to the right of the stage. She motioned for Ruth and Hattie to follow her.

With no other choice, they did. It was a secret passage…an escape route. Why would Fanny help them?

They hurried after her, down a narrow flight of stairs, into a basement of sorts. She opened a large wooden door, ushered them in, and closed it behind them. When Ruth's eyes grew accustomed to the lack of light, she could make out barrels, crates, packages, and one other person in the corner.

It was Giovanni Zapelli.

He sat in an old leather armchair, curled up like a little boy, staring straight ahead. There wasn't even a flinch of a muscle when they burst inside the room.

"What is going on, Fanny? Why are the police here?" Ruth dared to speak first.

"Coppers. You may have noticed we deal in illegal liquor, ladies. Surely, you knew that when you came down to the docks. Or are you really that naïve?" Fanny scoffed.

Hattie pointed to her brother. "What's wrong with him?"

Fanny wrinkled her nose. "He has spells. Always has. I let him think he is the big boss of this gang, but the truth is…I am."

"You are?" Ruth looked at Fanny in a different light. "You run the club and the rest of the operation?"

"Sure, I'm the strong one. We've never known what causes these spells of his. Freaks out at the sound of a gunshot. Everytime. Goes into a sort of a trance. He'll be like that for a couple of days. When he comes out of it, he don't even remember. Picks up like nothin' happened." She plopped down on an old stool. "I have to have everything accounted for 'cause I never know when he's gonna go off. Left up to him, we'd all be in the big house by now."

Hattie settled on a crate next to the stool. "Why did you save us? You could have just let the police take us down to the precinct."

"Sure, I could have done that, but I like you. I been thinkin' Ruby here could take my place as the entertainment. Leave me more time to run the business. Somebody needs to keep these louts in line."

Ruth continued to stand and stare at Fanny. "You want me to sing? All the time? In your club?"

Fanny cocked her head at Hattie. "What, is she daft? That's what I said, isn't it?"

"There is only one problem," Ruth said.

"What is that?" Fanny replied.'

"My name isn't Ruby."

"Not Ruby? What are you talkin' about?"

Hattie stood and rushed over to Ruth. "Hush, you don't know what you are saying." She smiled at Fanny. "Of course her name is Ruby. She's a singer. That's what she does."

"No, Fanny saved us. She deserves the truth. I don't care what she does. Deep down, I know Fanny is a good person," Ruth continued and addressed Fanny.

"You love Moose don't you? He is your man—the one you want, the only one."

"Sure, that's right. What's it to ya?" Fanny answered.

"Well, I have a man. A man I love so much, I'd die for him. Do you love Moose that way?"

Fanny looked up at Ruth, her eyes filled with tears, and her voice turned soft. "Yeah, I love him like that. When the gun went off and caught him in the shoulder, I thought he was dead. I nearly collapsed." Her face filled with understanding. "Who's your man, honey?"

"No, Ruth, don't." Hattie warned.

She went on, "It's okay, Fanny understands. My man is…his name is, Peter. Peter Kirby."

The room remained quiet as they waited for Fanny to register what Ruth said.

"Peter Kirby, the man upstairs with Captain Adams?"

Quietly, Ruth assured her. "Yes, Peter. He's my fiancé. Your brother took him from me on our wedding day." She dared to touch Fanny's sleeve. "You wouldn't have liked that, would you, Fanny?"

Fanny looked down at Ruth's hand. "No…no, I woulda got real mad."

"He's my man, Fanny. My one true love. The man I want to marry. Giovanni took him from me."

"Took him…"

"Yes, I've come to take him home," Ruth said, her voice soft and low.

"You tricked us?" Fanny pushed Ruth's hand off her sleeve, gently.

"For the man I love. You would have done the same for Moose. We're women. We stand by our men. We'd die for them. Right, Fanny?"

Fanny sat down with a thud. "I thought I had you figured, thought you were good girls. Turns out, you're like me, after all. Well, it's too late. Peter refused to take care of Moose's wound unless we let Captain Adams go. I ordered Mac to take them down to the river."

Ruth choked. "To the river? You're going to shoot them?"

Fanny didn't answer, she stood suddenly. "Moose, he's upstairs in a bedroom. The police will find him. I have to go to him." She raced to the door.

"Wait, what about Peter? Where are they…"

Cal came in with the police raid, George right behind. He watched as the police gathered the patrons that didn't escape and load them into a paddy wagon. The girls were not in sight, and Cal began to panic. He raced up the stairs, burst into every room, until he found the room Moose was in. He grabbed him by his shirt and shook him.

Moose yelped.

"Where are they? Where are Hattie and Ruth?" Cal yelled.

"I'm shot, I don't know nothin'. Can't you see I'm hurt?" Moose whimpered.

"I'll mess you up even more if you don't tell me where the women are." Cal shook him until he cried out.

"Alright, alright. I don't know any Hattie and Ruth. All I know is there are two singers, Harriet and Ruby. Fanny took 'em."

"Leave my man alone."

Cal froze as he heard a gun cock behind him. He dropped Moose gently down on the bed and turned.

Fanny walked into the room, gun pointed at his head. "That's better." She waved the gun toward the corner chair. "Get over there."

Cal obliged, but watched her carefully. "The police are downstairs, miss. They'll find you. This man can't move. You need to give yourselves up."

She bent over Moose. "You okay, sugar?"

Cal watched as the two lovers crooned over each other. "Where are the girls, miss? Where is Peter Kirby?"

Fanny seemed content to fuss over Moose. "The girls are downstairs in the basement. Peter and the good Captain are on their way to the river…to be shot."

Stunned, Cal only hesitated a second, bounded down the stairs, and found the passageway to the basement; the hidden door was standing wide open. At the bottom he could see a heavy wooden door, open, and rushed in only to find the room occupied by a single babbling man in a pinstriped suit. No help there. He rushed out and into the street.

Ruth and Hattie ran toward the docks. The shadows danced around in the moonlight distorting everything whether moving or inanimate. Ruth thought she saw a group of men moving something down at the edge of the river.

"We have to catch them, Hattie. Hurry."

Hattie panted after her. "We don't have guns, Ruth. Let the police get them."

"There's no time. They'll kill them before the cops could get there."

"Wait, Ruth, listen. Someone is coming behind us."

In the distance, back toward The Blue Feather, a male voice called out.

"Look, Ruth, I think it's Cal." Hattie turned and left Ruth standing alone.

Hattie ran to Cal, and Ruth hesitated. She looked forward at the docks and back at Cal running toward them. His voice was louder now, shouting something and waving his arms.

A gunshot rang out. Ruth screamed and ran toward the river.

The gravel rolled under feet making her lose her footing. Rocks dug into her knees and the palms of her hands, and ripping her dress. She scrambled to her feet, ignored the pebbles embedded in her skin and continued to run toward the sound of the shot, footsteps pounding behind her.

A large delivery truck blocked her view of the dock. She rushed around it and stopped in her tracks at the scene. Peter and Captain Adams were on their knees, hands behind their backs, heads bent forward. A burly policeman stood a short distance behind them, gun trained on a crumpled body directly at his feet.

He glanced at Ruth standing beside the front of the truck. "Stay back, miss. I'm not sure he's dead."

In a weak voice, she called, "Peter?"

The burly cop winked at her. "They are okay, miss. I got here in time." He gave the body a stout kick. "Anderson, come over here and untie these poor blokes hands."

On the other side of the truck another policeman stepped out of the shadows. "Right, boss."

While Anderson freed Peter and Adams, the first cop bent over the body. "He's dead. The others were rounded up by Murphy's division. I think we're safe here."

Ruth ran toward the river.

Peter stripped the last of the rope away from his wrists and met Ruth half way. The embrace was urgent, passionate, and unrestrained. They clung to each other sobbing.

Cal and Hattie arrived, breathless and smiling.

Finally, Ruth pushed gently away. "I was so worried, Peter. You could have been killed. Thank God the officers arrived in time."

Peter's face clouded. "What are you doing here...dressed like that? You were on stage — singing. Frankly, I had no idea about this side of you. I'm not sure, I can accept it."

"But, Peter, I..."

A siren interrupted her answer. The black and white came to a screeching halt, spinning gravel, the siren's song fading like a dying swan. Another cop jumped out. "I need everyone here down at the station, pronto. Everyone needs to give a statement. I have room for three."

Hattie and Cal pulled Ruth towards the open door. She protested.

Peter turned to Adams who hadn't moved since his hands were untied. He was visibly shaking. Instead of following Ruth, he clapped a hand over the captain's shoulder and said kindly, "Come on, old man. You can ride with me." They both turned away from Ruth and slipped into the second police vehicle.

Ruth couldn't believe Peter thought she had betrayed him. All she wanted was a chance to explain she was there to save him. He hadn't given her the chance…but he held her, squeezed her so tight she couldn't breathe, nestled his face in her hair. He loved her, she just knew it.

On the ride to the station, Cal tried to reassure her. "He'll be alright, Ruthie. It was a shock to him. To see you on stage, dressed like that, singing to a brawling lot of drunken men. I'm not sure I could have understood that, either. Seeing Hattie dressed like a common, well…it was enough to cause an apoplexy." He patted her hand. "He'll come around."

She turned to Hattie. "I want to get my other clothes, Hattie. I don't want him to see me in this again. Please, can you ask the officer?"

Hattie was directly behind the driver. "Sir, can we make a stop before we go to the station? Ruth's dress is ripped; she wants to be decent to give her statement. So do I, for that matter."

"It's against policy."

"Please, for decency's sake? Think if it was your mother, or sister, please sir?"

The officer didn't speak at first, but he slowed the vehicle. "Well, just this once. Where do we need to go?"

Hattie directed him to the fish market down the block.

"Make it snappy," he warned.

They hurried to the back of the store and tried the door. It was locked. "We'll have to try the window." Hattie went around the side of the building.

Ruth followed, glancing around to make sure the policeman didn't see them. A small window was the only entrance on the side of the building. Hattie was already half way through the unlocked opening, wiggling through inch by inch. She dropped on the other side and poked her head through to address Ruth. "Wait here."

"Guess we'll be dressing out here in the alley," Ruth said aloud.

In less than a minute, Hattie was back through the window, clothes tucked under her arm. "Hurry," she ordered and stripped off her red gown.

Both girls stuffed their costumes into the empty bag and headed to the other side of the building.

Ruth felt more comfortable as they sped through the city. *Thank goodness for sensible Hattie. I never would have made it without her.*

The officer ushered them into an empty room, but Ruth saw Peter's blond head through a window across the hall. He wouldn't look in her direction.

After their statement, Cal steered them outside to the automobile. Ruth looked everywhere for Peter, hoping he would be there waiting for her. He wasn't.

The house was dark when they pulled to the curb. Ruth knew he had to pick up his mother. Surely, he would wait for her. She bounded through the front door. Sarah stood in the hall by the stairs.

"Where is he, Sarah?"

"He's gone already, child."

"But, I need to talk to him...explain."

"He told us what happened. You messed up, Ruthie. Give him some time." She pointed to the stairs. "Now, go let your ma know you are in one piece."

Ruth whispered to the little maid as she passed. "I'm sorry—I wanted to save him, Sarah..."

"I know, little one. Go on, your ma and pa are waiting."

Her footsteps echoed down the hall, but all she heard was Peter's choked whispers calling her name as he buried his face in her hair.

Chapter Thirty One

Ruth would turn eighteen in one month. A lifetime had slipped by in the last few weeks, transforming the girl reflected in the mirror into a woman way before her time. The silver plated brush slipped through her glossy black hair with ease as she contemplated the changes in the family, the changes in her. Time was ticking by, she should be putting the finishing touches on her toilet, but emotion welled in her chest. Through it all, she could still hold those dear to her, hear their sweet voices, and revel in their presence. It could have turned out much worse. Now, she examined the tiredness in her eyes and the paleness of her cheeks.

The rouge pot sat unused in the top left drawer of the vanity. She pulled open the door and reached for the pretty little container. The lid screwed off without effort. One finger hovered over the creamy concoction, hesitant, cautious, and thoughtful. This time, she would take a moment to contemplate the consequences. Her parents would admonish the reckless decision, Sarah would scold her, and worst of all she could lose Peter forever. Such a small thing, insignificant, really, but it had always been the subject of numerous arguments with Mother. She forbid her to wear it, afraid it would label her as cheap, easy. Sarah raved about Ruth's alabaster skin and applying artificial color would dampen its natural illumination.

Last, there was Peter. The look on his face the night of
the raid said it all. Yes, everyone advised against it,
and she almost listened to them, almost. Instead, with
eyes closed, she dipped her finger into the jar and
dabbed a tiny, tiny bit on each cheek and smoothed it
gently into her skin.

Ruth would never be the same again, never be the
innocent girl of a couple months ago. It was her choice,
now. Mother would have to accept it. Sarah, well,
she'd have to remember her place. Peter? Oh, Peter…

She shrugged off the worrisome thoughts.

A soft, quiet red lipstick subdued the subtle color on
her cheeks, and she allowed herself a smile. Satisfied,
Ruth slipped off the favorite comfy robe and donned a
white lace dress hanging on the open closet door.

The clock struck the hour. Sunlight made the
puddles on the pavement below sparkle like diamonds
after the rain, and through the curtains, she watched
Cal Taylor's brown coupe come to a stop at the front
curb. He was here to collect her—usher her into the
next phase.

If he noticed the rouge, long practiced manners
prevented him from commenting. He offered his arm
and escorted her to the auto.

After making sure the skirt of her dress was
properly tucked inside, he bent to kiss her lightly on
the cheek. "It's a beautiful day, and you are beautiful,
as well."

"Thank you, Cal. You have been such a good
friend."

A comfortable silence fell between them as Cal steered toward their destination. The landscape rushed by, and the tranquil atmosphere allowed her mind to contemplate the past few days, undistracted.

The day after her statement to the police, there was a knock on the door. Sarah was at the grocer, her parents were resting in their rooms, and it was left to Ruth to answer the door. There had been no word from Peter, but she bounded down the stairs, still hoping he would see his mistake and come for her. It wasn't him. It was Fanny. Fanny Giovanni.

"Hello, Ruby...or should I say Ruth?"

She hardly recognized the woman. The only clothes Fanny ever wore were flashy dresses made for stage performances. Even in the kitchen, she donned a large apron to cover the spangles and beads. However, here she stood, dressed in a lovely brown suit, gloves, and a pill box hat. A total transformation. "I...I thought you were in jail, Fanny. What are you doing here?"

"Bail, honey. I got plenty of money, remember?" Fanny looked past her into the foyer. "You gonna invite me in?"

"Of course, please, come in." Ruth opened the door wide.

"Mighty nice digs ya got here. Never would have figured it of little ol' you. You played your part real good." She swept inside and headed for the parlor. "I wanna talk to you. Private like."

Just when I thought this all was over...what can she want from me?

Ruth indicated the settee, and Fanny sat down.

"Would you like some tea? Sarah is out, but I would be happy to fix you a cup, myself." Ruth really didn't want to leave Fanny alone, but offered anyway.

"No—no tea. I need your advice and your help," she began.

"My help? I don't know what you mean, how can I help you?"

Fanny straightened the skirt of the suit and cleared her throat. "I want to be a lady, you know, like you."

She stared at Fanny. "A lady? Me?"

"Yeah, I mean, yes. Captain Adams...well, he showed me something. How a lady should be treated. I ain't much of a lady, but I wanna be." Her face took on a dreamy look. "It felt real good to be pampered."

"Captain Adams...but I thought you were in love with Moose."

"I am." She paused. "You see, part of my agreement with the judge is that I go straight. Make the club legit. Stop runnin' booze, that sort of thing. I love to cook, so The Blue Feather is gonna become a dinner club. I want Moose to be the manager, but he probably thinks I am just a dumb dame. I want to show him, prove to him I'm the real brains behind the operation."

All this was hard for Ruth to take in. She heard the words, but it didn't make sense. "What about Giovanni? Won't he object?"

Fanny laughed. "We fooled 'em all for a long time. Who would take a dame seriously as a mob boss? I let my brother be the front man. Kept everyone in line to think he ran the show. He's got issues. Blanks out. I set all this up and have been runnin' it from the beginning. Now, I have to go legit or go to jail. I have to prove I can go straight. You're gonna help me. I need Moose." A crimson shade transfused her face. "Not only because I love him, but I need his protection from the other rival gangs. They want what I got—and will take it from me without protection. Moose will find somewhere else to go if I don't snag him."

"I don't know anything about a dinner club, Fanny." Ruth shook her head.

"I got that part figured out. I saw the way it was between you and Peter. That's what I want for Moose and me. Besides, I want you to be the main attraction. I want you to sing."

Ruth hung her head. "Oh, no Fanny, I could never sing in a club. I haven't heard from Peter since that night. He's upset because he saw me singing—in front of all those men."

"He doesn't know why you were there?" Suddenly, Fanny stood up. "I'll fix it. Leave it to me." Before she bounded out the door, she shouted over her shoulder. "Don't worry; you're as good as walking down the aisle."

As unexpectedly as she appeared, she disappeared and left Ruth standing in the open door wondering how in the world Fanny Giovanni was going to 'fix it'."

But, she did.

The little coupe arrived in front of the boarding house. It was quiet, no one out front. Ruth looked at Cal. "Did he change his mind?"

"Go on in and see for yourself," Cal answered.

Everyone was there, her parents, Sarah, Hattie, and even Fanny and Moose, all smiles. Cal whispered in her ear from behind. "Go on, he's waiting."

Eager and hopeful, she stepped through the back door into the garden. Peter stood dressed in a black suit, smiling, eyes a twinkle...blond hair slightly fluffed from the breeze.

A slight shock rippled through her at the sight of Captain Alexander Adams standing next to him.

Mother touched her arm. "It's okay, Ruthie. His wife is here, and Ella. The past is the past. Mrs. Adams is a lovely woman.

"But Cal should be..."

"Look again, Ruthie. He is."

Ruth turned back to the front in time to see Cal Taylor squeeze between Peter and Captain Adams, taking his place as Best Man.

Father took her arm. Hattie straightened the short train of her dress, and handed her a bouquet of red roses. The piano played the first strains of the Billie Holiday song 'It Had To Be You'. Ruth closed her eyes letting the music wash through her. It stirred the very soul, filled every fiber of her being with a slow, rhythmic pulse, and she wondered who chose the song. When she opened her eyes the song was over, and the introduction to the traditional wedding march began. Ruth took a step toward her future. As she did, something caught her eye. On the white runner leading to her waiting bridegroom, in front of Fanny Giovanni —a single object...a single blue feather. Fanny just smiled.

THE END

Made in the USA
Charleston, SC
30 September 2012